CHILDREN OF THE LIGHTHOUSE

By

Ila G. Lee

ISBN: 1-4033-6098-7 (e-book)
ISBN: 1-4033-6099-5 (Paperback)

Library of Congress Control Number: 2002094104

This book is printed on acid free paper.

Printed in the United States of America
Bloomington, IN

1stBooks – rev. 1/9/03

Table of Contents

Front cover photograph: Cape Argo Lighthouse, 1920.
Back cover photograph: Cape Argo Lighthouse, 1995.

Table of Contents

Front cover photograph: Cape Argo Lighthouse, 1920.
Back cover photograph: Cape Argo Lighthouse, 1995.

First letter:
"Grandpa" = Harmon A. Powell; "Grandma" = Minnie Ellen Demerest Powell
Grandpa Powell was a member of the "remnant" (Romans 11:5) who died in 1932.
Harmon and Minnie Powell's children were:
1) "Aunt" Luella 1886 (husband Ed Metcalf)
2) "Uncle" Warren Powell (wife: Myrtle) 1889
3) "Aunt" Daisy (husband: Bee Taylor) 1894
4) "Aunt" Opal (husband Fay Elliott) 1896
5) "Mom"= "Ruth" 1899 (husband Wyman Albee = "dad" 1893)
Second letter:
"Cousin" Ralph = "Aunt" Daisy's son, who was born about 1911.
"Cousin" Lewis = "Aunt" Luella's second son, who was born about 1912.
Harmon Elliot (born about 1918) = "Aunt" Opal Elliot's son.
Old man Metcalf = "uncle Ed's" dad
"The store" (pages 2 & 4) was grandpa Powell's store at Charelston, Oregon.
Frank Wyman (related to Etta Wyman Albee)
Linda (don't know relationship)
"The babies" = Ellen and Lavinia
Third letter:
"Grandpa Doc" = Ed Metcalf's father\Coos Bay\Old timer
Old Brown? (unknown identity)
Vi? (unknown identity)

Chapter I

Cape Argo

Cape Argo Lighthouse Residence 1932

The Grand residence at Cape Argo was three stories high, four stories if you counted the basement which had half windows at ground level.   Here was the laundry room with electric washing machine, a double cement laundry tub used for two rinses, and one with bluing in it to brighten the clothes. Each machine load had to be sent through the wringers attached to the washer on a swivel. When on the left, the clothes from the wringer dumped into the first rinse then it was swiveled into the center of the two tubs where the wrung out clothes dumped into the bluing rinse. From there they went into the basket to be hung. There were clotheslines in the basement, out in the yard and in bad rainy weather there were lines in the attic a really long haul but necessary when crews were being housed. Mom always warned us not to play with the wringer, be careful, but at least on one occasion Ila got her fingers caught and pulled through to her wrists before Ruth could wham the release. No serious damage was done to her hand.

On the main floor there were steps down from the kitchen to the side walk which went out to the tower. To the left of those steps was the basement stairwell. The kitchen was where the mainstream of life unfolded, for in cold weather (which was at least nine months of the year) here was the main source of heat. The latest model of wood cook stove (also the government supplied coal) did its job of heating water and house.

Behind the stove were the water pipes that carried the cold water through the firebox, then into the hot water tanks. Back here the dogs and cats would sleep together, soaking up the warmth, forgetting all hostilities.

Mom was expecting a visit from a lady, she could just as well do without. The woman wouldn't control her three year old. He was known to bite other children and Ila and Allen were afraid of him. The little dogs and puppies and cats had to be put in the basement for his and their protection. Trix wouldn't put up with any mistreatment from any child. That's why she was *mom's* dog. She never drew blood, but it was scary. The two big cats, Sunny and Thunder, would be limp as dishrags when picked up unless hurt, then they could bite and scratch worse than Trix.

Mom and her friend had barely settled into a nice cup of coffee and social amenities when Ila let out a scream from behind the stove. She and Allen had gone, where no child was supposed to go, to get away from the beastly kid. Ila got a three inch burn on her arm from the hot water pipe.

Wyman and Ruth felt like they were raising two families. Ellen and Lavinia were born only eighteen months apart. Then it was six years before Ila's birth and Allen's two years plus one day later. Dr. Horsfall attended each birth using the dining room table as a delivery table.

When Lavinia was about two, and just walking good, mom took her and Ellen out for a walk. Lavinia took off running down the railless foot bridge that connected the lighthouse rock with the mainland. Far below, the ocean crashed on jagged rocks. Ruth dropped Ellen's hand commanding, "stay here!" as Lavinia had started out on the bridge, delighted to be getting away. Ruth's cries, "Stop! Lavinia, come back!" only made her laugh and toddle faster to the bridge. Ruth was gaining on her, but as Lavinia turned back to see where mom was, she lost her balance and tipped over the edge. Ruth caught her dress tail, and swinging Lavinia into space, pulled her back up onto the catwalk. Mother was so shaken that she cried all the way back to the house. She had complained many times about the lack of a fence around the yard, and no railings on the foot bridge only to go unheard. This incident did carry some weight, and a fence was built shortly after.

Ellen and Lavinia loved to play dolls in their quiet sunny bedroom, on the second floor, with a partially slanted ceiling on one side by the long hipped roof. A four foot wall hid storage space where the roof met the floor. This was called the "cubbyhole." It also held the toy boxes which made cleanups quick. One time Ellen and Lavinia had gone camping with mom, dad and other relatives. After that experience, playing dolls became "camping." They put magazines, newspapers, toys and dolls into a heap in the center of the room between the two beds. Ellen found matches on dad's bedside table across the hall along side his cigarettes. Ruth smelled smoke, and began searching the main floor. Cousin Lewis was visiting. He traced the smell to the girls upstairs bedroom. The flames were leaping from the doll hair to doll, and paper was exploding into more flames. He grabbed a hooked rug from beside the bed, and threw it over the crackling heap. It smothered the dancing flashes, turning it all into a thick dark smoke. A few stomps and diligent crushing ended the flames. And water from the pitcher and wash basin on the dresser cooled the inferno bringing it into control. Where were the girls? It was hard to see in the smoke filled room. There, isn't that a crack in the door to the cubbyhole? Yes, yes, there they were, huddled together in that dark hole that could have been their death. Lewis urged them to come out, that the fire was out. By now mom had arrived to behold two very terrified sniffling little girls.

The lighthouse families subscribed to an unwritten code that the children were not to play together too much. At least habitual contact was strongly discouraged. There was an invisible line that divided the whole Lighthouse reservation in half for the respective families. Usually the children accepted it, and obeyed by not crossing over without the permission of parents. Once in a while Lavinia and Ellen would sneak out of bounds to play and talk to Robert Barker.

Lavinia loved to ride the little red wagon down a slope in the tall grass, or sit among the scarlet Indian-paintbrush that blossomed at cliffs edge. She was often found at the boathouse, which was on the land side of the little island, for the sun was warm, and the bank protected her from the cool sea breezes.

The goats gathered here also for a noon day rest, snuggling close to the warm ground. Oh, those goats! They could be a nuisance, but they also provided some of life's heartiest laughs. Nan was a black goat with a white tail which she would switch enticingly at anyone who followed her. She would always place herself at the head of a group of vacationers that Wyman would escort to the old lighthouse that lay in ruins on a part of the island that was fast being washed away by the relentless sea. Dad would warn, "Don't grab Nan's tail or she'll butt you." However, people would forget. Wham! Dad would have to pick them up, and shoo that goat away. Back she'd come to lead the way again. No one ever tweaked her tail a second time! Ruth had obtained the goats, feeling that milk was a very healthy addition to the family's diet. Ellen hated the goats, believing their milk was responsible for her being overweight. Ruth had seen Nannie butting Ellen, Lavinia or Ila to safety away from the cliff edges, when they were too young to know the danger, the same as she did to her own four legged offspring.

Allen was expected in April or May, but arrived in March somewhat premature. As other children were said to be brought by storks or left under a cabbage leaf, lighthouse children arrived on the wings of a seagull, doubtless in the midst of a sea storm. The medical profession was just beginning to recommend that babies have foods and liquids other than mother's milk. Dr. Horsfall suggested Ruth give Allen a bottle of tomato juice between feedings. He developed a high temperature, and the doctor said to give him plenty of liquids, and some more tomato juice. His fever climbed. It remained 107 for several hours. Ruth had to keep a pillow between him and her arm because he was so warm. In desperation she decided to quit the tomato juice, and try some mint sugar water. It worked! His fever started declining. Allen must never have tomatoes—they were poison to him. The allergies, and allergic reaction were not well known at that time. The fever left his black hair curled in ringlets.

Trix was a dukes mixture of small dogs. She was a yellow, short-haired dog about the size of a house cat. Her rather long ears stood straight up most of the time like a Chihuahua. She kept us regularly supplied with puppies. One pup, Peaches, became Ila's dog by merit of her protective attitude. Peaches was cream colored with a white blaze down her forehead. When sitting in Ila's lap, she would snap at anyone who menaced them. She never reached a year of age. Wyman had caught a salmon, and cleaned it on the edge of the cliff where the discards could fall into the sea or the sea gulls could eat it. Before he could wash the grass off with a bucket of water, Peaches licked up some of the blood. Deadly poison! She died. Lavinia played Moonwinks on the piano as a funeral dirge for the dog. Ruth gave Ila Penny to take her place.

Captain Harvey and his wife lived in a little cottage on the graveled road that led from the lighthouse to civilization, i.e. Charleston and the grocery store. Further on down this road was Empire, North Bend, and Marshfield. The Captain liked his booze, and for fun had a little dog (one of Trix's pups) which he had taught to drink beer. That dog was quite a clown when he got soused. After a good slurping of beer, Captain would coax him to jump into his lap knowing full well the dog would misjudge the distance, and fall in a crumpled heap on the floor. Up he would stagger, head in the wrong direction, then try again. Ruth was indignant, but Wyman had a good laugh. Allen and Ila couldn't figure out what was wrong with that dog, but if dad laughed, they figured the dog must be okay.

Ruth had been objecting to Wyman accepting Captain Harvey's offer to row him out to the freighter to pilot it into Coos Bay. He was the Harbor Pilot, the one who knew every rock, shallow and dangerous spot on the way in. He knew what tides to enter on, and where the treacherous tide pools spun. He would pay Wyman $20.00. It was a tempting offer, since a whole month's salary with the Lighthouse Service was only $90.00 or there about. Ruth would have preferred to go with out the extra money than to suffer all day long not knowing what his fate might be. He and Captain Harvey launched the eighteen foot row boat in the alcove north of the footbridge. The curvature of the rocks on both sides may have served as some protection from the winds, but from the banks above, the sea appeared to be sending breakers crashing onto the beach with as great a fury as anywhere along the shore. The two men watched the sea to get its rhythm. When it retracted, and sent only a small breaker ashore, they ran the skiff into the surf and jumped in. Each of them manned an oar, and started rowing as hard as they could, to cross the breaker line before the next huge wave could crash.

Ruth had observed these launchings from the bank above many times, this time in driving rain. Babe Allen was bundled against her chest in heavy blankets, and Ila clung to her coat tail watching her daddy disappear into the sea. For many minutes they gazed after the men seeing them appear at the top of each wave, then dip into a trough out of sight for much too long a time. By a half mile out it was impossible to tell where they were without the telescope. They had to keep the bow headed into the wind so that the skiff could ride up each new wave without swamping. They arrived at the freighter, El Segundo, without mishap. After seeing Captain Harvey safely hoisted into boatswain's chair up to the freighter deck, Wyman aimed the skiff toward shore and fought the sea alone for the return trip.

Meanwhile, Ruth turned away, heading for the little barn to feed the pigs and chickens. "Come Cecil," she called, "Come Sally." "Pig, pig, pig!" Sally came, leaving her piglets squirming, grunting and squealing in the hay lined brooder. While the pigs ate their slop at the trough, Ruth sneaked a very young piglet out of the nest to hold. It squealed as it left its warm comfort of the brooder. It quieted, even closing its eyes, as it reveled in having its back gently scratched. Ila was frantically yanking on mom's coat sleeve begging to hold the piggy. Ruth was reluctant, nevertheless, Ila's persistence melted her better judgment. So, handing piggy over, Ruth started to say, "Don't squeeze him." But already Ila squeezed a little too tight, and the piggy pooped. That was enough of that! Piggy went back to bed. She washed Ila off at the water faucet. She allowed the water to run on the ground for a while to moisten the Calla Lilly that grew there.

Ila had seen Calla Lilies once before at cousin Ralph's funeral. He was aunt Daisy's only child who died at age 26 of tuberculosis. They had visited him once when he was being cared for at the County Poor Farm near Coquille. There were Myrtle trees at the gate which opened to a long driveway that approached the home. Dad had to park the car outside the gate, then walk the long way up. A tick fell from the trees right into the top of Ila's head. Several evenings later, Ruth was mending clothes at the sewing machine. Ila was whimpering for no apparent reason. Ruth coaxed her over beside her, and just happened to place her hand on her head. "What's this? What have you got into your hair?" she asked. Well, Ila didn't know. A tick! She and daddy removed the mean ugly bug from under the skin with tweezers and kerosene.

Mama used to cry often over Ralph's dying so young. She cried over aunt Daisy too, who died before him with tuberculosis. Ralph would hitch hike from California to Charleston. En route he would find fine wood which he would carve into chains. He carved one chain with a skeleton box attached with carved ball inside all from one piece of wood. He gave dad a gift of a handled cup with a ball attached by an eight inch string. You tried to catch the ball in the cup.

Aunt Daisy and uncle Bee Taylor had moved to California searching for a living. The Great Depression hit, and made it even more difficult to find work. Grandpa and grandma Powell were going broke, because of the depression, trying to run their little grocery store at Charleston. Grandpa had preached the Kingdom of God to all who came to his store, and he lived by its principles. He would not refuse credit to the poor families who came to his store. Finally he sold out, and with a few belongings, he and grandma bought a lot next door to aunt Daisy in California. They put up a little frame cottage covered with tar paper, and thus joined the many peoples who survived the depression in tar paper shacks. After much tribulation, grandma died there.

After Ellen and Lavinia started school Wyman became a likely candidate for the school board at Charleston Elementary. A couple of times he was voted president. He was a stickler of getting the three R's into the kid's heads which was more important than any new fangled methods the colleges were putting out lately. Also, the older teachers were stricter disciplinarians. The three R's and good discipline equated with more brain power for the kids. The majority of the board agreed, so the older teachers were retained. One young teacher filled a vacancy. In the spring all eight grades put on a festival. Ruth volunteered to bring trillium to cover the lattice work that formed the backdrop for the children's stage. This took armloads which were readily available. Oregon had suffered many burned areas which seemed to be ideal ground for wild trillium to grow. One of these meadows was under the limbs of a new growth forest, which was located in a spot on the way to Charleston Grade School. The stems of the trillium were easily fifteen inches long, the green leaves at least eight inches form tip to tip protecting the delicate white blossoms. They filled the small schoolroom theater with their sweet, woodsy fragrance unequaled by any couture perfumery. Little girls danced around May poles braiding satin ribbons on the pole. Little boys played elves, and choruses of youthful voices sang the songs of America's original composers.

A favorite game at recess was Anti-I-Over. All the children were divided into two teams—sometimes even the teacher played. They usually chose a captain who took turns choosing teammates. One team started the play by tossing the tennis ball over the schoolhouse roof where the opposite team endeavored to catch the ball. Actually the ball was sort of rolled up the roof so that the ball would barely make it over the peak, and gently roll down the roof to the waiting team. (Throwing the ball high and loosing it was grounds for being kicked out of the game were it deliberate.) The catching team would quietly, but swiftly race to the other side of the schoolhouse and whoever they tagged became a member of their team until all children

were on one team. The team with the most members when the bell rang, signaling recess over, was the winner! By the way, when throwing the ball up the roof, if it didn't quite make it over the top, the throwing team would cry "Pigtail!" each time until the ball went over and down the other side. Often times when changing sides around the schoolhouse, the teams would crash into each other causing a wild mili. On one such occasion one of the bigger boys ran into Ellen, and the two went sprawling in the grass like a toothpick and a butter ball. Everyone laughed so hard they could hardly make it back to class.

When the summer season brought low tides on the ocean's shores, Wyman would organize a family mussel bake. Early in the morning before the sun could warm the rocky island cliffs, Wyman would row the boat along side the mussel encrusted rocks, and scrape the huge mussels into the boat with a rake. These rocks were farther out to sea than the lighthouse. They were the hidden ones, which at high tide, caused the breakers to curl and foam. On the beach below the boat house, family and relatives were heating a big caldron of hot water to a boil. When the mussels arrived they were dumped in for a short boil, and some vinegar was added. How delicious! Cooking them turned them a bright orange color. Their shells were blue and black, and were six to eight inches long—a size rarely found today. The children played on the beach all day—in water and/or out of water. Ellen could float on her back, and paddle out by the huge seaweed covered rocks that enclosed the beach. Ruth became alarmed, for she herself was deathly afraid of the water—even wading was a challenge. "Ellen, you come back here!" Well, Ellen made a big turn, and paddled back to shore much to Ruth's relief. Aunt Luella brought thick heavy cream to the picnic to go on the strawberries that Lewis and Grace brought. Uncle Ed and Ted brought beer for the men. There was always lemonade and homemade bread with tons of butter. Donald was collecting little black crabs from under the rocks. He would then turn them loose in the warm sand, and he would called it his crab farm. Someone caught him throwing them into the boiling water for the mussels, and Ted threatened to tan Donald's hide.

At the end of the day, everyone headed home. It had been one of those beautiful gatherings where everything went well. Why was Ila whimpering then? Ruth had nursed Allen, and had put him to bed.

She now looked at Ila. Her face looked blotchy. She lifted her dress, and there on her tummy and back were big red hives. Ila was allergic to strawberries. Too bad. No more strawberries for Ila.

Ruth gave Ellen a birthday party at the beach. This was in July. Ruth went early to arrange the picnic, and hide candy bars in the cracks and crannies of the driftwood for the children to look for later. Later, the guests were hidden in tall grasses around the place where Wyman would bring Ellen in the car. Out she rushed, starting to dash to the beach when everyone jumped up crying, "Surprise! Happy birthday!" Her feet nearly stopped midair in amazement. She had forgotten it was her birthday. They played tag, and Simple Simon Says, found candy bars, ate picnic and cake. Then Wyman built a warm beach fire as the sun set. Over on the rocks the lighthouse twinkled its beacon. How fun it was playing hide and seek as darkness grew. Sometimes the beams from Cape Argo helped you find someone. Then you could warm up at the fire, and roast marshmallows. By ten o'clock the party was over. All the children squeezed into the car, some on another's lap, to be driven home.

The light stations were always in a state of update. Cape Argo's mammoth prism was turned by kerosene power until government crews switched it over to electricity. It took a few months to make this change over. The crews had to be lodged by the keeper's families. An extra $20.00 was granted which they could keep as wage or hire help. Ruth needed help badly. Wyman drove over to the Days to ask Mrs. Day if she'd like to help Ruth do laundry, and fix meals for the crew. He wore the lighthouse uniform. Babe Day answered his knock, and with wide eyes disappeared inside yelling, "Mama, a policeman! Daddy, a policeman!" The Days were petrified. They had a small still in the dugout cellar where Mr. Day made a little moonshine for family and friends. Many needed it for medicine. Who told? What a relief when Mrs. Day opened the door to Wyman. Mrs. Day was happy to have the work. She could bring Babe with her.

Babe and Ila were playing in the window well where coal was delivered. They started throwing coal chips and dust at each other. Before they were found, two little children had coal dust in hair, on lashes and down their neck. Oh, those black faces! They had to bathe, and stay in the house for the rest of the day. When Allen learned to walk, he and Ila would play in the swing out by the clothes line. Ruth could keep an eye on them from the kitchen window where she washed the mounds of dishes. Suddenly, mother rushed out of the house, and grabbed Allen into her arms just as the fog horn blasted its first bellow. Allen would get hysterical if the fog horn started when he was alone. Ruth had glimpsed this heavy fog wrap its way around the tower heading for the house and shore.

Wyman had taken over his father's job of lighting the range lights on the Coos Bay bar after Ira, his father, was drowned in a skiff wreck on the bar. He applied for permanent Lighthouse Keeper, and was accepted. Shortly after he and Ruth were married, the service sent them to Destruction Island, Washington, then Robinson Point on Vashon Island and back to Cape Argo. It was nice to have spent sixteen years here among relatives and friends before the service started transferring the family around. Now they had to pick up everything, and move to Turnpint, on Stewart Island in the San Juans.

Packing everything meant exactly that! Even the linoleum from off all the floors, had to be loosened, and rolled up. The two cows, Pet and Beauty, were sold as were the pigs, Cecil and Sally. Some of their piglets were given away. Ruth was tired of puppies so she swapped Towser for Penny as Ila's dog, and gave Penny to Lewis.

Lewis drove logging trucks. This was rough, dangerous work. Sometimes he hid Penny inside his work jacket, taking her to work with him. Out on the road he turned her loose in the truck cab where she would stretch up trying to look out the window. How she loved to see new places, and smell new things coming in the truck air vents. At lunch time she went back into his jacket. Then in the restaurant he would unzip his jacket when no one was looking, and out popped Penny's head ready for bites of donuts or hamburger or bread. The other drivers would tease, "Hey Lewis, is that a big flea you've got in your coat?"

As each piece of furniture was crated, the house developed an empty sound. A wonderful library of National Geographic magazines had to be left behind, the Watchtower and Golden Age collection were given to Luella, and mother said we wouldn't need the Christmas things anymore. A large moving van would collect our furnishings, and deliver them to Bellingham. There they were picked up by the Coast Guard's lighthouse tender. Dad accompanied the furnishings. Ruth drove to Portland, where we had hotel reservations for the night. The "City of Roses" suddenly appeared as the car crested a final hill. There below lay rows and rows of three armed street lights, necklaces of golden lights, twinkling lights scattered all over like heaven come to earth.

Once in the hotel, mother made us notice where the fire escape was, just in case. Tomorrow she would drive to Friday Harbor, where she and the children would catch the mail boat to Stewart.

Chapter II

Stewart Island

Stewart Island, Turn Point Lighthouse (1935-1936)
Ship in background: Empress of Japan

Wyman arrived at Turnpoint in late July. He had walked the approximate two miles to Prevost to meet his family, and help carry baggage. They were arriving on the Chichawana, which carried mail and passengers to Stewart Island at least twice a week. It was a sturdy little fish boat, privately owned. It had picked up Ruth and the children in Friday Harbor by pre-arrangement. Deck side was cold and blustery, so Ila was seated next to the little coal stove in the engine hold. Too bad!! She was prone to motion sickness, even when riding in the car. Oh well, the coal bucket was conveniently positioned beside her. "Land ho!" was a welcome sight. So was daddy. It was wonderful to be with him again.

Old Light Stand 1935

The dock at Prevost was a long one. It reached out to deep enough water to allow the boats to dock. Once the family stepped onto the dock, they could feel the sun warming the road to home. Everyone felt cheerful. Allen and Ila skipped along the dusty trail, while father explained things he'd heard about the inhabitants of the island to mother. How someone at one time had a model A that could travel this meager trail clear to the lighthouse. But Stewart was only two miles wide and three and a half miles long, really not practical to bring a car to. Besides, the roads were basically trail, hardly wide enough in a great many places for a car.

Turn Point 1935

Finally we came around a curve from under the trees to an open view of the sea. Just below and to the right nestled the lighthouse and its accompanying residences. The northern half of the dwelling would be ours, since the Clements were already in the southern half of the two story home. It was much like a duplex—each residence had its own front and back doors. Wyman showed his family through the house. He showed Ruth their bedroom, and he allowed Ellen, the oldest, to choose which bedroom she wanted. The remaining one was

Lavinia and Ila's. It was the sunniest and coziest. Ila was especially happy to be teamed up with Lavinia, for she could never forget that Ellen made her fall out of bed in the dark night at Cape Argo. She kept pushing her away, because Ila snuggled too close, and she couldn't sleep.

Wyman, Ellen, Allen, Ila, Lavinia (spring 1936)

Ellen was bossy too. Lavinia would share a doll with Ila, but not Ellen. Oh, Ellen and Lavinia's dolls were the most beautiful in the world. They took such good care of them, that for years their little dresses were still crisp with the sheen of new cloth. And their shoes were so perfect—white with one strap to button and oh, the silver buckle ornament! Ila's doll was "Shirley," Shirley Temple of course, and if you had ever asked her she would never have traded Shirley for any other doll, even Ellen's. Shirley had dimples and golden curls, and since the original dress was lost, she had to wear real baby clothes which didn't quite fit right. And her shoes were missing, not to mention those shiny knit stockings. Ila played with all her dolls a lot. One was a boy doll named Johnny. He had a yellow jacket and green Dutch pants. He really belonged to Allen, but Allen preferred cars.

The lighthouse tender arrived in the sunny afternoon with two foot swells and winds off of the Straits at ten to fifteen knots. This was ideal weather for the sturdy tender, but it took him a lot of skill and coordination to transfer household furniture and foods into the skiff. Disaster hit when the derrick controller let the sewing machine down into the surf where the skiff had been. A big wave had tipped and separated the boats at just the critical moment. Everything else was delivered to shore without mishap. The sewing machine worked, but seemed to give mom trouble from time to time. The salt water couldn't have done it any good.

Our neighbors were Assistant Mr. Ed Clement and his wife Bessie. Mr. Clement had a nervous disorder, maybe shell-shock from serving in World War I. Bessie was Scottish. The Clements were from Coos Bay, as we were, so it was a renewing of old friendship. They were a childless couple, but vulnerable to children's charm. Allen discovered that playing within sight of their kitchen door elicited cookies. Allen suggested to Ila, "Come let's go play cars in front of Clement's kitchen. The sidewalk makes a good road, and Mrs. Clement might call us to the door, and give us cookies." He was right. We had barely arrived, when the door opened, and this plump, smiling, apron fronted lady beckoned us with cookies: "Come, would you like some cookies?" "Umm, thank you," we chimed through mouths full of sweet goodness.

The Clements had a dog named Zero. He was black, had long wavy hair, and retrieved. He would swim into the icy-cold water after a stick or a rock splash. We were cautioned not to do it unless an adult, mainly Mr. Clement, was watching. The tides and currents could be treacherous around the point sometimes creating whirlpools that could spin a rowboat in circles. A doggy could be swept way out, and not have the strength to swim back.

Turnpoint Lighthouse on Stewart Island was the most isolated of stations that Wyman served at after he became a family man. There was a small grammar school there. It was one room where all eight grades were taught by one teacher, Mary Mordhorst. She was Charlie Barnhardt's aunt. School was sweet. Mary wanted Ila to attend the class as a kindergartner to encourage or challenge the boys, Arthur Rassmussen and Charlie Barnhardt, to have good attendance, and apply themselves in first grade. All eight grades were in one room about fifteen by twenty feet. Roy and Grace Rassmussen were in 7th grade with Ellen and Lavinia. Mary arranged a play of Columbus discovering America. And she arranged for the class to sing songs like Old McDonald Had a Farm and America. As fall turned to winter, Mary would have a fire going in the little wood heater by the time everyone arrived for class. A tea kettle simmered there to provide warm water for washing hands and faces and for tea or soup. The toilet was an out house used alternately by boys and girls alike. There were few unnecessary trips, for young ones didn't like that cold drafty hole.

Ruth and Wyman had celebrated their last Christmas at Cape Argo, they thought, the year before. They had been baptized as International Bible Students in 1916 (later named Jehovah's Witnesses), the year after their marriage. The Bible Students had determined that it was unchristian and hypocritical to continue celebrating the Winter Solstice in the name of Jesus and his birthday. By a few simple applications of mathematics to the historical records in Luke surrounding Jesus' birth you can arrive within a couple of weeks of his birth in the fall of the year. Despite Wyman's explanation of his decision to not celebrate Christmas, the Clements kept begging Wyman to allow them to throw an old fashioned Christmas dinner for us with gifts for the children. Wyman's tender compassion for these loving folks who never had children of their own, and the fact that he had loved Christmas for children's sake, caused him to break the resolution this one time. The occasion was lovely and memorable. Allen received a windup train track set, which spouted sparks from the stack like 4th July sparklers. Ila's gift was a little wicker rocking chair. She spent many hours rocking dollies to sleep in the years that followed. The chair was indispensable when playing "house." Ellen and Lavinia received sparkling zircon bracelets.

The Mordhorsts ran sheep on the island. The sheep left wool on the bark of trees, on barbed wire, on the brush. When out for a walk, Ruth would collect these tufts, bring them home, and wash them. Then with help of a couple of cards obtained from Montgomery Ward, she would card the snowy wool into soft fluffy squares. They eventually became the filling of a tied quilt, more like a comforter.

One winter night produced an unforgettable electrical storm. Ruth awoke the children in the middle of the night to witness this magnificent display of wonderment. Jagged lightening stokes with simultaneous thunder balls danced before us threatening trees, residence and lighthouse. Mordhortst's sheep had been grazing on the cap of the cliffs about a half mile northwest of the point. With the first sudden crack of lightening and thunder, some of the sheep leaped off the cliff. At least one met its death in the foaming breakers below. One landed on a shelf where it was rescued come daybreak, but another was washed off the cliff's abutment by the rising tides and endless breakers. A piece of driftwood caught in the ragged rocks looked like a sheep and had Allen fussing for days for dad to go get it.

As the storm began to fade away, long fingers of the Aurora Borealis began to stretch, and rotate in the northern sky. "Look Ila, look Allen, the Northern Lights!" Mother exclaimed. They are rarely seen this far south. Truly, this was the first time Wyman or Ruth had ever seen them.

Another time that winter, a moth was once sighted. The National Geographic had run an article on this particular type of moth, which helped Ruth identify this clumsy lovely creature. Ruth had stayed up to keep watch with Wyman until the midnight shift exchange. They caught this huge moth battering its wings against the porch light. She placed it in a large soda cracker box to show us the next day. Daylight seemed to mesmerize the insect for it didn't care to fly, and it just clung to Ruth's finger walking round and round with wings spread upward above its back. Forward of the wings were the feathery antennae. Underneath the wings was a fat and short body covered with a black line, a black dot inside the upper wing tip, circled in white. Also, there was that iridescent blue-green gold woven in the pattern. He looked as though he had the strength of ten butterflies.[*] That evening Ruth released him to continue his life cycle and perpetuate his kind.

---

[*] This is apparently one of the many varieties of the so-called Showy Emerald moth whose scientific name is Dichordo Iridaria. Varieties of this moth appear in various shades of green. Its habitat is in south and southeast United States, and would be very rare to spot on the west coast.

The radio kept us abreast of the news in the outside world. Lavinia enjoyed the day to day episode of "Little Orphan Annie" devotedly looking up the clues to tomorrow's adventure on an Annie's decoder. These were elaborate metal gadgets about the size of a policeman's badge with a center wheel which revolved the single letters of the alphabet through little windows as you turned it. By following the instruction at the end of the program, you could spell out the words of the clues for tomorrow's episodes. And don't forget to drink Ovaltine which produced the silver (like coupons) to send in for "Orphan Annie" shakes, mugs, and decoders. The radio did not take over our lives as the TV can today.

Ruth read aloud chapters each night from the great American epics like "The Last of the Mohicans" and "Uncle Tom's Cabin." From these we learned to love and respect these noble races of people whose lives might touch ours before our life's journey should end. Those authors had a genius for wrenching tears from the reader. Often mother would have to hand the book to father to finish reading aloud a chapter depicting the demise or catastrophe of these grand people.

Danger was a common companion to those who lived on the lighthouse. Here at Turnpoint there was no doctor. The closest one was in Bellingham or Friday Harbor. Both of these places were miles away by sea. Ellen became sick with some kind of dysentery one winter here. She maintained a high temperature for several days. Just as dad decided to go get a doctor, her fever broke and she was on the mend. Allen also had a high temperature and convulsions—an allergic reaction to tomatoes. We knew they were like poison to him, it was accidental that he got some from some canned Campbell's beans. Since mom had been through this with him before, she handled the situation well, cooling him in a bath of cool water. Whereas the first episode of fever had made Al's hair grow in curly ringlets, this second attack took half the curl out.

In the spring, Mary had us clear the school yard of dead branches, leaves and ferns. She prepared a place away from the woods where they were burned. Ah, how the sweet fragrance of smoke curling in the sun warmed air, mixing with the perfume of the purple wood violets and yellow Johnny Jump Ups! Some time during the spring, that rare American orchid called the Lady Slipper pushed its way above the mosses on the forest floor. It sends up a single snapdragon type of blossom. Of course, there were acres of wood lilies edging the fields in every direction.

On the south of the point, the keepers had chosen to throw away the trash. The cliff fell sharply down to high water line then sloped to the edge of a fifty foot drop off. The keepers stood at the door of the engine room, and threw the junk in the direction of that cliff, later to be thrown over cliff's edge. Wyman had placed a piece of the engine outside the door to be cleaned and later replaced. Allen picked it up and said, "Dad, can I throw this over the cliff?" "Yes," he said. So over it went as far as a four year old could throw. It landed below water's edge, but still visible. When reassembling the engine, Wyman realized what he'd done, and went looking for Allen to determine appropriate discipline. But no way! Mr. Clement had witnessed the whole episode, and forbid father to lay a hand on his son. Wyman then had to rig a pole with hook on end which he spent the next half hour fishing, and groping for the elusive part.

Cement platform is cistern cover

There were two old cherry trees growing by the work shop. That spring, they burst into bloom like fruit trees in the "Garden of God."

There must have been plenty of bees for the trees produced over a hundred quarts of cherries for both keeper's wives, and they barely looked touched. Raccoons visited regularly to stuff themselves and their offspring with dessert. One night Zero and our dogs, Trix and Towser, cornered a raccoon at Clement's place where the cement steps came down from the sitting room. Someone threw a fish net over the hapless coon, and the next day he became a permanent resident of a chicken wire cage. He was soon to be joined by coon number two, caught on a fishing trip that dad arranged with Ila and Allen. The sun was out, the tide was low, and Puget Sound looked like glass—not a ripple. The raccoon decided to abandon the rock where he was eating mussels, to swim ashore. Dad simply dipped him out of the water with the long handled fish net. Then he was transferred to a gunny sack, which we brought to put fish in. Soon he learned to gently pick cherries and crackers from our fingers. It's funny how each morsel had to be dipped in water first. I don't think anyone really knew the sex of these two raccoons. Surprisingly they could share the same cage without fighting.

Two hapless raccoons

One Sunday Mr. Clement chose to go fishing on the rocks below the lighthouse. Wyman joined him after checking all the lighthouse equipment, and signing the log. Herring were jumping and Ed had already pulled in a perch. They were deep in conversation about the good old days when something rattled the clam shells they'd broken up for bait. Climbing out of the sea behind them was a gigantic octopus. "My God, Albee, let's get out of here!" They retreated in haste to the tramway steps, fish lines dragging. The animal slid back into the sea, disappearing in a cloud of blue-black ink. This episode was food for news, and excitement for months to come. Other occasions of fishing from these rocks were accomplished with wary eye on the rocks behind them.

Wyman planned a family trip to Friday Harbor to shop. He had to order groceries to last the winter which the Lighthouse Tender would pickup, and deliver. Ruth, Ellen and Lavinia would visit the beauty salon for permanents. Before leaving Turnpoint, Wyman gave Ila and Allen a half dollar each to spend in town. Ila had a little leather coin purse with a chain handle to put her half dollar in. Allen put his half dollar in his pocket. Thereby Allen was tempted to play with it. So he fingered it, and took it out to look at it. Soon it was under the floor boards of the outboard skiff just out of reach, stagnant sea water sloshing over its silver tail. The day had dawned in all its glory with cloudless sky from horizon to horizon, and the waters of San Juan De Fuca Straights reflected the blue sky like a looking glass. Wyman was pleased with himself for choosing such splendid weather for this excursion. He was anxious to make the round trip before the tide changed, and the evening breezes rose. They enjoyed a family lunch, then went their separate ways: Allen with dad, the three girls with mom. The trip to the beauty salon limited the amount of time Ruth would spend window shopping. So, a quick trip to the dry goods shop for dress material, and odds and ends at the ten cent store had to suffice. Wyman and Allen saw the barber, ordered the winter supplies for both keepers, and went to check on the brand new Chevy he had to store while living at Turnpoint.

The Chevy was a black four door sedan, one of those intermediate models that sometimes occurs when last year's models are evolving into the next. It was a 1934-35, and had only been driven about 800 miles when mom drove it into storage in Bellingham. The proprietor fell head over heels in love with that car. He wanted to buy it. His final offer was exactly the same price, dollar for dollar that Wyman had paid for it. But, no sale! Dad also considered it a prize, and wanted it to be waiting for him when his tour at Turnpoint was over. Its differentiating feature was an add-on baggage trunk in the back, called a carry-keen. It unlatched at the top, and unfolded into an open carry all. It was being well cared for in doors, up on jacks.

Already it was time to meet Ruth and the girls at the wharf for the return trip. A few urgently needed supplies were loaded. Then everyone was assigned a seat for an even distribution of weight.

Leaving this Harbor was pleasant until crossing the shoals into open water. By now there was an escalating chop on the Sound. Before the trip could be completed the sun would be set, darkness impending. Stewart Island had lost several residents in identical situations, even fish boats designed for open sea had sunk in a surprise gale near the island's shore. With the skiff loaded to the gunnels with family and belongings, Wyman ran the outboard full throttle the whole way, which amounted to a three knots per hour creep. Clement had the light blinking merrily as they landed safely on the rock shelf at the end of the tramway. Ed lowered the tram on the rails which extended under the water so Wyman could maneuver the boat onto it. Once secured, up she went. Wife and kids eagerly disembarked, and climbed the wooden steps up to the wooden walkway that connected the lighthouse to the residence carrying their most precious belongings with them. The rest of the supplies went with the boat up the tram where it was easier to unload.

The lighthouse service asked Mr. Clement to move to the Smith Island Light Station. If you stepped forward to the edge of the front porch at Turnpoint, you could see the Smith Island light blink its code at you from the south. Ed would have preferred to remain under Wyman as Keeper, because he was just, fair, truthful, kind and honest. He had declared once, "Wyman, I love you—but I hate your religion!" He was promoted to Keeper, and transferred to a light service where it was necessary to row a boat out to the range lights to light them. They were kerosene powered.

An especially bad storm broke just at sundown which was lighting time. It was allowable at this particular station to wait for severe storms to break into manageable seas to attempt lighting. But his sense of duty compelled him to go. Bessie begged him not to. The assistant keeper begged him not to, and perhaps others, but they could not restrain him. They knew as they gazed after him he'd never make it. Before their very eyes, the boat swamped, and it was days before his body was washed up on a beach miles away. That evening at supper dad announced, "I have good news for you kids, the next assistant keeper has four children. His name is Pederson. I don't know the ages of the children yet." We were delighted with the expectation of close companions. The "God is great and God is good" grace was said with more then usual zeal.

Allen was still struggling with the potty training at four years old. He always seemed to remember right in the middle of dinner after everyone had settled down comfortably. Someone had to help him— Ila was elected. He was the cutest baby brother anyone could ever have. She was indignant and hurt once when mom accused her of not loving him, because they were quarreling. Thereafter, her conscience always bothered her when they had a noisy disagreement.

**Wyman, Mr. Pedersen, Ruth, Ellen, Jensene, Lavinia, Evelyn, Jens Jr.,
Ila, Allen, Tootsie (Bernice)**

Mr. Pederson was a rolly polly Scandinavian. Jensene Nevada was the oldest, Evelyn next, then Jens and Tootsie (Bernice) the youngest. Jensene and Ellen invented a secret club in which they made beads from colorful papers. Once pasted and dried they were coated with fingernail polish, and strung on a string for a necklace. Evelyn and Lavinia were partners in their counter club, and Jens Junior sort of drifted to where ever the action was. Allen, Ila and Tootsie were a fond threesome. Sometime after their arrival, Ellen and Jensene had a disagreement which turned physical when Jens hit Ellen. Lavinia, always quick to shrink from hostilities, did not join the fray. Ellen had to hold her own against two. This led to less association and more rules to respect between families living next to each other.

Back row: Wyman, Mr. Pedersen, Mrs. Pedersen
Front row: Jens Jr., Allen, Ila, Evelyn, Lavinia, Jensene holding Tootsie, Ellen

The lighthouse tender (The Fir) arrived with the winter supplies for both families, and with them, orders and contractors to replace the old wooden structure (that housed the light) with a small cement base. This light was electric, fed by a generator inside the engine house.

The crews did not have to be housed by the keepers. They slept aboard The Fir. It took only two to three days to complete the job. The keepers gave them pleasant ado, but perhaps with some reservations at loosing this link to civilization. The sole contact with civilization was by mail out of Prevost on the Chickawana.

The new light stand

The Rassmussens invited us to dinner one evening. The three mile trek was full of fun as Roy and Tom Erickson hid in the bushes, and jumped into the path just as the girls approached with a big

"Booooh!" The girls screamed while the boys retreated in a jumble of laughter. Mr. Rassmussen was a fisherman by trade. He owned his own boat. They told us the history of Stewart Island and the cause of death of some of its inhabitants buried in the tiny grave yard up by the school. A three year old boy had died when the button on his bib overalls had cut his chin, and became gangrenous. One winter there had been so much snow and cold that each family had to sleep all together in bed to keep warm. One family even had the dogs sleep on the bed to help keep them warm during the night. The dinner established bonds of friendships and hospitality that lasts to this day.

Ellen, Lavinia, June, Grace, Roy, and Tom played Pit and Flinch. Allen and Arthur played cars and trucks and someone's doll made Ila happy. Arthur was so clever, he was showing Ila the way to his home after school once. After leading her a little way off the path to a very sunny, mossy clearing, he checked on his rabbit snare he'd made with a stake and wire. There didn't seem to be any bait or special effort to lure the rabbits. Rabbits probably hopped around heedlessly, like uncle Remus' famous rabbit, carelessly hooking a hind leg in the loop.

Fall in the San Juan Islands is most beautiful. The alders and maples turn to their gold and red colors amidst the evergreen fir, pine, spruce. The pathway to Prevost or to the cemetery and school were carpeted with falling leaves and years of collected needles. You just don't see this landscape, you breathe it in deeply, imprinting the aroma of this painted woodland on your senses to time indefinite.

It was the kind of day that would spin a web of beauty on the annals of time. Ruth headed to Prevost to pick up the mail, with Allen shuffling along beside. Trix and Towser ran joyously ahead up the leaf covered path that climbs up from the shore. Half way up the hill a wild jack rabbit, disturbed by the commotion, dashed out of hiding, and went leaping up the hill just ahead of Towser. How fortuitous for Towser, or was it? His nose was so close to the bunny's tail that already he felt the pride of a grand hunter upon him. But alas! The bunny kicked out with two hind feet so hard that Towser ended up in a crumpled heap at the bottom of the hill. He picked himself up, shaking dirt and leaves, tail drooping, rabbit nowhere in sight, and mistress laughing at him—the greatest clown on earth!

Allen and Towser overlooking Prevost Harbor

About a mile before Prevost, Ruth turned on a fading trail edging its way up a craggy mound, which provided a panoramic vista of Prevost Bay. She could see the vale where Mordhorst's had a few cows and a bull. And farther west she could make out bits of the Olympic Mountain Range presenting their lofty peaks above the gathering mist of winter. Al stood in profile in bib overalls and French tam, gazing in wonder of this majestic view against a back drop of infinite blue sky.

Trix caught sight of a large orange rabbit. The contest was on. She was a spunky dog which fearlessly pursued rabbits clear in to their dens. Being part Rat Terrier and Chihuahua, she was precisely their size. This was a very dangerous preoccupation, for at least on one occasion she couldn't turn around or back out of the tunnel, and we had to walk two or three miles home to get a shovel, and go back to dig her out. Not this time though. The rabbit was a domestic one gone wild and was bigger than Trix or Towser. So when Ruth coaxed her, she came back out.

Shopping spree's were accomplished with the arrival of the new Montgomery Ward's catalog. Mom drew Ila's footprints on a piece of paper, and ordered her first black patent leather Mary Janes. Dad ordered a candy bucket (a galvanized water bucket full of Christmas hard candies). Oh, how pretty all that candy was! He also ordered a wind-up mantel clock with chimes, as a birthday gift for mom.

The shoes were tight on Ila, but she absolutely avowed that they were not. Ruth hoped that they would stretch enough with wearing to be serviceable. The next school day dawned revealing a three inch snowfall during the night. Everyone looked forward to attending school in the snow. The walk was three miles up tree covered lanes, through a cow pasture, then a short cut through the barn yard where huge turkeys gobbled, fluffed feathers, and often chased these timid human intruders. Just past this point, the trail climbs uphill on the final grind to school. It was here that a water blister on Ila's heel broke. She began to cry, and refused to walk. So Ellen had to carry her piggy back up the hill. Ila would never hear the end of that, because after school Ellen and Lavinia had to take turns carrying her home. Half way home, Ellen ordered Lavinia to run the rest of the way to get dad to come and carry her home. Dad was a most welcome sight. Ellen was relieved of her burden, Ila was relieved of Ellen's irascible scolding.

That winter was a severe one. The keepers only realized after the near zero weather set in, that the cedar water tanks that the government had built should have been drained. Setting above ground fully exposed to the elements, the water froze, and the tanks cracked. As the water seeped out through the cracks, it froze in long, wide sheets and pillars two to three feet thick. The water in the tank was fed by a pump, the source of a natural spring in a ravine just past the reservoir. The adults carried water buckets from the spring to the house until the weather broke, the ice thawed and the tank repaired.

Cedar water tank

Here it was spring again. Ruth took Ila rowing and fishing. It was another of those lazy-hazy days when Puget Sound was behaving like a calm, protected lake. She rowed northwest below the cliffs where the sheep had fallen, then around an abutment to a cozy little inlet. Here Ila's fish line began jerking and yanking. Among squeals of delight and excitement she pulled the fish in close enough to the boat for Ruth to dip it into a net. Behold! The fish was a pretty pink. Could you really eat it? Its face was ugly with a couple warts and a whisker sticking out of each side of its chin. Yes, you could eat it. It was a Ling-Cod. It weighed about four pounds. Ruth was pleased.

One lovely day the waters straight out from the point were acting funny. There were a lot of little spinning funnels coming up from the depths, bringing fish to the surface, which just floated around limp, as if they were too dizzy to swim 'round like fish. We tried to catch them with our hands, but when you squeezed, they would wiggle out and away, drifting again in circles. Had an earthquake underwater caused it?

As the island path leveled out from behind the houses, heading towards Prevost there was an overgrown swamp or small lake evident. Wyman gathered the family together to clean out part of it for a safe swimming pool. The project was never finished for he received a request from the Lighthouse Service to go to Yaquina Head, Oregon for a building program there.

Chapter III

Yaquina Head

Yaquina Head Light Station (September 1937)

By the opening of school in September of 1937, the Albee's were moved into their residence at Yaquina Head, Agate Beach, Oregon. This tower was of the tall, picturesque type with 114 stairs in the staircase that spiraled to the lens room. It's height was eighty-one feet.

Unique to this lighthouse was a giant mound that towered a few feet above and behind like a mysterious backdrop on the eastern skyline. A barbed wire fence curved its way up nearly to the top and across from South to North marking the reservation boundaries. This hillside is ablaze with the colors of the coastal wildflowers all summer long: Goldenrod, Queen Ann's Lace, Indian Paint Brush, Iris, wild Sweet Peas, Oregon Grape, Daisies, California Poppies, blue and white vining Vetch and Bachelor Buttons, to name a few. A child could snuggle down among their stems escaping the cool sea breeze, warming body and soul with sun's rays.

On the south side of the point, the ocean had carved a small rocky beach. The rocks averaged in size from one to four inches in diameter. They were ground smooth and round and hard. They bounced like rubber balls when thrown hard against each other. Ellen and Lavinia were allowed to take friends down to this beach to show them the bouncing rocks and the interesting displays of sea life in the tide pools. Everyone had to be careful of throwing the rocks for sometimes they had a mind of their own—bouncing back at you or sideways or would shoot right straight up.

When the Miller family visited us, we took them down on this beach. They were from inland, Springfield, Oregon. They were thrilled by the thundering surf, the many colored seaweeds and sea life. Their father was a railroad man so he made a good living for his family. The mother was ambitious for her daughters to become missionaries at the Watchtower School of Gilead in Brooklyn, N.Y. She helped them in their full time ministry and in time they qualified and graduated in 1943. They were both assigned to the same foreign country. Maxine married there and her husband became the head of the Interpretation Department. Fern became ill and in time returned to the U.S., and died of cancer. Fern very patiently taught Ila to sew doll dresses. Ila had a set of six ceramic like dolls with moving arms that needed dresses. Fern sewed and dressed three or four, while Ila learned how to hold and push a needle, make stitches, and tie knots. By the end of Fern's visit, Ila believed she could sew anything.

Allen, Ila, Bob, Ellen, Lavinia, Maxine, Fern Miller

Aunt Luella and uncle Ed along with cousins Donald and Dewey drove up to Yaquina Head from Charleston one lovely summer day. Neither family would inform the other that they were coming to visit. So often times they would meet on the highway between destinations. Therefore, both parties would survey oncoming traffic to avoid the disappointment of arriving and finding no one home. If they met midway, they could turn aside to a park, and have a family picnic.

Having arrived, cousin Donald took Allen out on the cliffs overlooking the sea's breakers. He had brought along his home made slingshot. The "Y" was fashioned from a sturdy alder branch, with a half inch wide band of tire inner tube tied to the arms with twine. Seagulls and terns were swooping and sailing in the stiff ocean breeze tempting this eleven year old Nimrod with their casual glides. To a five year old, Al, the adventure was exciting. When they returned to lunch, Al could hardly wait to announce to everyone, "Donald was out tootin' teagulls with a ting-tot!"

The parking area had been covered with gravel from Agate Beach only three miles away. It was easy to find moss agates amidst its ruts. Sometimes you'd find a traveler's dollar bill entangled in the stems of tall grasses along its perimeter. We collected agates and sea shells here in myriads of kinds and colors. Lavinia would make pipe-cleaner people and animals of shells and stones. Allen and Ila sold them for pennies, nickles and dimes from off the steps of our home. These visitors called Allen curly top and Ila freckles. After teasing they would buy something, then follow the walk way out to the tower where one of the keepers would escort them through the engine room and up to the lens room where they could walk the cat walk completely around viewing the horizon in every direction with unobstructed view.

Behind the living room door there was a favorite built in settee with a hinged top. Inside mom stored extra blankets, or sometimes Allen and Ila would hide there when playing hide and seek.

Twice or three times Ruth entered this room to find total strangers resting in father's favorite stuffed leather arm chair, or rocking gently in her rocking chair. Mother would stand or sit, nervously fidgeting, trying to maintain a polite attitude until the intruders would take leave. I suppose she locked the door, for awhile thereafter, but it wasn't convenient to open it to family every time they wanted in. Besides, if father was coming in to dinner or supper or changing shifts I'm sure he wouldn't wish to walk clear around the house to the kitchen entry.

That winter, Allen and Ila came down with hard measles. Therapy in those days was to keep them down in bed with the shades drawn, a blue or green painted light bulb placed in the bed lamp and hot water bottles of heat to bring out the measles in full force. The idea was to draw out as much poison as possible which built up a strong immunity to any future contact with the disease. It seemed to work. Neither kid got damaged eye sight and neither ever got the measles again, of whatever variety.

During the measles episode, one of the most furious storms hit the coast that had ever occurred. The sea sent wave after foaming wave crashing on the rocks and cliffs below the lighthouse. The hurricane winds churned the sea into a froth then blew gobs of huge foam balls over land and sea, covering everything in sight like dirty snow.

Ellen and Lavinia started high school at Newport. They were both freshmen and the school was exciting. Ellen desired to go to college. On her own, she signed up for the courses that would lead the way to that possibility. She got a "D" the first semester of French, but somehow worked her way up to an "A" before leaving that school. Ruth and Wyman would not consider sending her to college. They wouldn't show partiality among the children. Too bad, because none of the rest had any interest in higher education anyway. Ellen could have made it with a little help.

Newport High was one of the first schools in the nation to offer a course in Driving Education. Ellen passed the course, but not without at least one hair raising incident. Ruth had to shop for groceries one night so Ellen used this opportunity to practice driving. Ila wheedled a chance to tag along. The car was in the garage between the fence and the cliff which dropped about 200 feet into the sea. Her foot slipped off the clutch, and she tromped hard on the gas. The car whipped out the garage in a half circle. She braked and killed the motor with the rear bumper only inches from the cliff's edge. Earth and time stood still for several moments before we recovered enough from the shock to proceed up the one way cliff side to the twinkling lights of Agate Beach.

Wyman took the whole family to the high school football games. We all rooted wildly for the home team. Ellen especially enjoyed these excursions. Her school, Newport High, needed a song to represent them at the ball games so the music teacher rewrote the words to Harbor Lights, a popular song that year. Our family was very impressed with her genius. To this day the melody stands for Newport High for us.

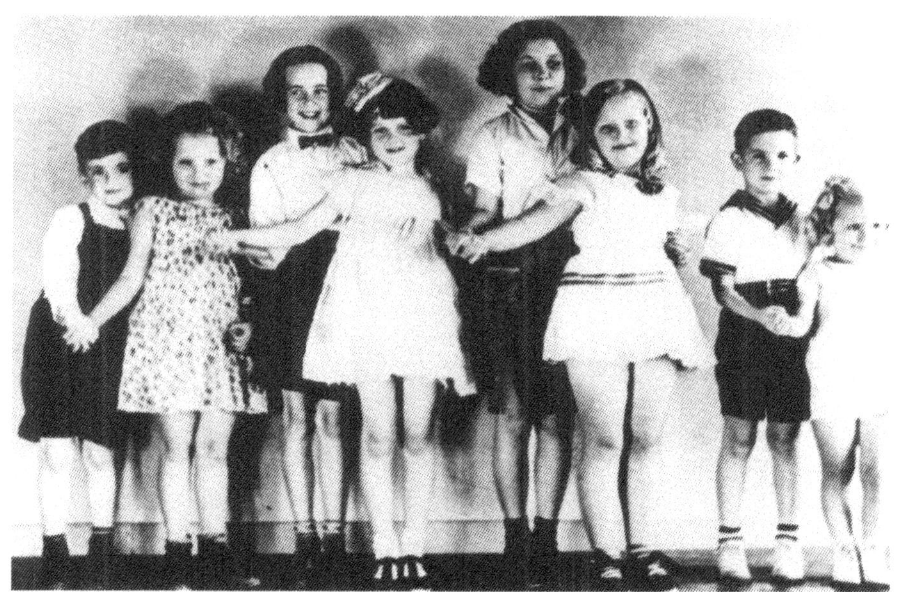

Newport dance class 1937

Ila's second grade teacher at Newport was one of those old maid school teachers that had survived from the turn of the century somehow. She was tall and skinny with raven black hair pulled back tightly into a bun at the nap of her neck. Her face was a noble nose with high forehead, piercing black eyes, but nicely shaped ears. Her skin was leathery and deeply lined like the grand Indian chiefs of the west coast. One time, she came flying out of nowhere in class planting a large hand on each of Ila's shoulders shaking her very resolutely. "I told you to color the turkey brown not orange. You pay attention!" Shocked and stunned Ila complied meekly.

Newport School class (1937)

Every once in a while the movie theater would present a picture to collect food for the poor. The school encouraged it by reminding the kids and parents to send a canned vegetable or soup or whatever as admission fee. Then whole classes marched from the schoolhouse door to the local movie theater to see a film about America, the beautiful.

The high school students put on a play near Halloween time. It was scary, of course. There were murders and haunted houses and much running around the stage by these thespians. All the grade school classes were allowed to attend the play on school time. They walked several blocks to the high school. Someone opened a closet door and there hung two human heads on the wall making faces at the audience in various conditions of red paint which ran down the wall. To the second graders it was sufficiently exciting, suspenseful and terrifying.

The government was adding wireless radio to the stations. Crews arrived along with truck loads of steel to build a radio tower. They set it solidly to the south of the lighthouse. Its ugly framework married the beauty of sea and skyscape. There were special connecting braces that were missing, yet they continued to build it over Wyman's protest and letters to headquarters reporting the defect. He declared that it would buckle with the first severe winter storms, and of course it did. The wind crumpled it in half right at the change of the midnight watch. Wyman heard it crash behind him as he stepped into the engine room where Mr. Zenor was bundling up to return to his residence.

Buckeled radio tower (fall/winter 1937)
New residence between keeper's home and lighthouse tower

One afternoon, as the bus arrived to take the little ones home from school, every one was pushing and shoving to be first in line to get on the bus. Barbara Church fell with one leg caught next to a giant tire that already had quit turning from the driver's slamming on the brakes. Pale of face, he leaped out of the open door kneeling by Barbara. He lifted her away from the wheel, and carried her over to the grass. Someone brought the first aid kit, and cleaned her scratched up knee and leg with alcohol. Her face was wet with tears, but everyone was greatly relieved to find that the wheel had not actually rolled over her leg. The wheel had only pushed and pinched her leg along. Even though these children were only first to fourth graders, this tragedy had a long lasting effect. Thereafter, orderly quiet lines prevailed when the bus arrived.

Barbara and Ila became best friends. She lived two miles from the lighthouse, quite a distance for two seven-year-olds to cover and maintain a friendship. Barbara's mother drew a paper doll for Ila. She also drew a dress to cut out and fold onto the doll. It was Ila's first and only paper doll—it became a keepsake.

Wyman had been spreading the Gospel around the neighborhood, and one of Barbara's neighbors invited him to have Bible study in their home using the guidebook, "The Harp of God." There were several children present: Barbara, Wesley, Ila, Allen and another neighbor boy. There was a great rustling of Bible pages as each child tried to be the first to find the scripture cited. Then dad would choose a child to read aloud for the group.

One beautiful July day, Wyman planned a trip to Toledo, the county seat. It was a shopping trip to check out the department stores that Newport didn't have, to buy shoes, etc. for the family. The sun came forth with vigor that morning turning the farmer's dewy fields into sparkling prisms. We stopped at one farm to pick up vegetables for winter storage. The farmer wasn't advertising so we just stopped and asked if he had extra to sell. He was pleased and happy to share his extra for a small profit. By afternoon Toledo's temperatures were pushing the mid nineties. Ruth, Ellen and Lavinia were at the beauty shop having permanent waves. Wyman took Allen and Ila to the drugstore fountain and ordered three chocolate milkshakes. The children had never had it before. How refreshing, how delightful! Then mother arrived and began rushing us so she could leave. What began as earth's greatest treat ended in disaster. Allen cried because his drink was snatched away. Ila suffered in silence as great gulps of icy froth pained her throat and gave her a headache.

Assistant keeper, Mr. Zenor, had two nieces visit for a couple weeks. They were about ten and twelve years old. Having made Ila and Allen's acquaintance, they started telling a never ending daily episode, "Hairy Monster from the Sea." Strange how the story was so like the real thing. There was a little girl and boy (brother and sister) whom the hairy monster caught after it came up out of the sea. The slimy green monster put them on a moving belt that was drawing them toward a circle saw where they surely would be sawed in two…However, the girls were called away before the story could be completed, leaving Ila and Allen forever apprehensive over the little brother's and sister's destiny.

Keeper's residence and natural mound

Gardenor's ran a little grocery store at Agate Beach. Coming from the lighthouse it was on the left as you arrived at Highway 101. Father would often stop there for items we had run out of between major shopping tours. He would search his pockets for pennies or nickels to give Ila and Allen for candy. Oh! What a pleasure! What fun it was to agonize over a penny's worth of cinnamon candies or a whatnot, or a jaw breaker, or a huge piece of bubble gum. Great day it was if there was enough of each kind. Sometimes dad would say, "Now hurry up, don't take all day." Mr. Gardenor would say, "Aaah, let them take their time. I can wait."

Wyman told Mr. Gardenor that already the Lighthouse Service was transferring him to Umqua Lighthouse at Winchester Bay, Oregon. There were about two weeks of school left in the school year, and he hated to cause Ellen and Lavinia to change high schools with only two weeks to go. Well, Mr. Gardenor wanted to help the girls for that short time. He only had to arrange it with Mrs. Gardenor who agreed. Leaving Lavinia was very questionable, for she was very timid and very attached to mother and family. Lavinia agreed to stay though, and as she was about to be a sophomore, everyone concluded that perhaps she had outgrown the close dependency. It did not come to be so. In a few days Ruth had to drive up from Umqua to get her. She was so lonesome she was in tears most of the time. She *did* finish taking her final tests at Reedsport High. Ellen finished at Newport High, ready to start a new year at a new school.

Chapter IV

Umpqua

Umpqua River Lighthouse (1938)

What a gorgeous place to live! The lighthouse tower was just tall enough to send the rotating light beams out to sea above the tree tops that protected the residence from the sharp ocean breezes or storms. Beyond this belt of weather gnarled firs, spruce, pine, huckleberry brush and salal, you stood on the edge of a half mile of deep, flowing, clean sand dunes. From the ridge, you could take a flying leap landing half way to the bottom of a sandy ravine causing a whole hillside of sand to move downward with you. In the bottom of the ravines were little yellow sand flowers and sometimes hard damp sand. Quicksand was possible and children could get lost in the miles and miles of dunes. Children were forbidden to go beyond the first ravine into which you could see the bottom from the edge of the woods. If Allen and Ila went the half mile out to the ocean, they had to be accompanied by Ellen, Lavinia, or mother. Otherwise, the first dune provided hours of delightful jumping and sliding.

Sand dunes at Umpqua

On the back side of the residence was a small swamp. Swamp grass made islands through it and previous dwellers had abandoned a four by five raft on swamp's edge. There was a board missing, but with a nice broomstick for a push pole, Allen could invent great adventures of the sinking of the North Star or the wreck of the Hesperus. The raft would not go far, as it would hang up on the bunch grass. The water was knee deep so a spill off board made wet muddy pant legs, socks and shoes.

One fall day, dad was cleaning this area up, scything the grass and dead ferns, and raking them into a fire pile. The dead dried ferns made wonderful arrows or whips for a game of cowboys and Indians. Ila borrowed Allen's pocket knife, and carved the end of a fern into a sharp point. Ila would throw the fern like a javelin. It would sail through the air and land sharp point sunk in earth, while the stem would continue waving until it was retrieved. Thus, imaginary buffalo were killed for dinner. Well, Allen got ornery and didn't want to play. So in a fit of provocation, Ila threw a fern straight at Al. My God! My God! The fern imbedded in his forehead just between the eyes. It hung there waving its three foot length as he stood there transfixed. He let a yowl, and dad grabbed the thing yanking it out. Blood trickled down his nose and face. Dad carried him into the house, washed the wound with alcohol and mechurochrome, and taped it shut with adhesive tape. There remained a half inch scar for years to come. A shocking reminder to never throw anything sharp at your brother.

This swamp was part of a rather extensive wet lowland that developed into a lake on the south side of the driveway. The whole family went down there to clean out a swimming hole on that lake. A large fallen tree, about 30 feet out, divided the swim area from the rest of the lake. Ellen was already swimming out by the deep water and log. Allen and Ila learned to place their chest on a six foot plank. By paddling hands and feet they could move the plank out to the fallen tree and back. Ruth was a bit discomforted by this.

By Halloween time, the Coast Guard was clearing property to the north, and was laying cement foundations for building apartments and offices for a full fledged Coast Guard Station.

Coast Guard residence being built (1938)

Knock out slugs from electrical switch boxes made terrific play money. Scraps of boards made building blocks for miniature cities. There was a cement goldfish pond in the center of the lawn. It was perfectly round, about two feet deep, three feet across. There were no fish in it, and Ruth wasn't about to put any in it. She didn't like it. It looked like a kid trap to her. Cousins Lewis and Grace drove up from Coos Bay for a visit. Three year old Janice, Allen and Ila were squatted around the fish pond dropping rocks into the murky water, watching them descend into oblivion. Janice grabbed a nice big rock from in front of Ila and plopped it in. Instantly mad, Ila gave her an angry push, and plop—Janice was head down in the pond. Brother and sister stood back in astonishment and frustration watching the poor child desperately thrashing the water with her hands trying to get hold of something to pull her head up. Ruth, watching out the window, came bursting through the door yelling, "Pull her out! Pull her out!" Oh yes, that's what she should do, but before either could act, Ruth was there pulling her up with a good grip on Janice's heavy winter coat. Grace stuffed her cigarette into her mouth, and received the terrified screaming child into her open arms.

Winchester Bay Elementary School was two small rooms. First through fourth grades were taught in one room. Fifth through eighth grades were taught in the other. Allen started first grade here, and was in the same room with the same teacher as Ila, who was in third grade. This teacher was pleasantly plump, good-natured, and helped you understand your schoolwork.

There was a boy in third grade who could spell the whole spelling list of words correctly if teacher called out the words in the order they were found, in the book. If she mixed them up he couldn't spell any of them. She discovered this before the year was out, and told him she wanted him to be able to spell them when she mixed them up. Did he have a photogenic mind? What became of him in life? He followed us home from school a couple of times, and we played cowboys and Indians. Mom didn't like him, because he didn't have bladder control, and she was afraid he had lice. She told him not to come anymore.

School ended in early June with a super field day at the Reedsport High School. Ila won the first prize, blue ribbon, in broad jump, which also included drinking a milk shake with the teacher. How pleasant a reward this was on such a warm beautiful summer day.

Our stay at Umpqua was too short. Already we were to be moved into Robinson Point on Vashon Island before school would start in the fall. Dad had his first automobile accident on leaving Reedsport that rainy night. An oncoming car blinded him as it flashed around a curve on this winding river highway. Dad hugged the bank too close. He stopped just short of a rock protrusion that could have crushed Lavinia's sleeping head. We had to return to Reedsport, put the car in a repair station, and accept the hospitality of fellow Christians—the Mills—for the night. In a couple of days, the dents were taken out of the car, the scratches painted, and we were on our way.

Chapter V

Robinson Point

A whole summer of vacation time lay ahead, allowing time to become familiar with new surroundings. Dad and mom had been here before, in 1919 shortly after their honeymoon at Destruction Island. We were delighted to renew old acquaintances with the Pedersens, who had arrived and settled before us.

Robinson Point (1939)

Robinson Point faced East. The sun rose from behind the Cascades and Mt. Rainier. About seven miles across the water was Redondo Beach, halfway between Seattle and Tacoma. People would come over in their outboards to pick up fire wood from the beach. The two dwellings were separate, but enclosed by a white wire fence. Inside the wire fence were lawn, lilacs, the wives' flower gardens; and on the north side of *our* house was a lovely old weeping willow tree. Beyond that lay a flat, extensive plateau that formed the Point.

Halfway out was a large Madrona tree under which someone had placed a swing settee. Beyond that was the lighthouse. A nice cement sidewalk encompassed both residences and connected the lighthouse several hundred yards away.

Past Pedersen's to the south, the sidewalk met the boat house and tramway that lowered the boats into the sound. This sidewalk provided many hours of roller skating for the children. By the time they would attend a rink, they were well on their way to ballroom dancing on skates. There were about ten acres to the reservation. Wyman would like to keep a cow, so he discussed it with Pete. If they both had a cow, the work involved would benefit both families. The first thing they had to do was build a cattle guard across the road at the entrance to the reservation. This allowed cars to pass through without stopping to open and close gates. The fence was attached to the guard on both sides. There already were a couple small barns. Each would repair his own. The cattle guard done, they could turn the cows loose to graze the ten acres.

Breakfast was a quickly grabbed box of Cheerios that was carried out to the beach. At low tide there were two sandy spits that etched their way out into the Sound right in front of the residences. Beyond the sand spits lay an underwater shelf of sandy shoals and seaweed beds which gave way to a sudden deep drop off. Allen, Ila and Tootsie loved to wade out here. They could dig clams with their hands. They learned where the sand dabs hid, half covered with sand, and warming themselves in the sunbeams penetrating the shallow water.

Ruth made fish spears out of broom handles and a nail driven in the end with the head removed. The children used these spears to catch the sand dabs with. They often caught enough for dinner, after they learned to allow a three to five inch angle to the death stroke. Another time they were carefully looking for sand dabs when the tide started coming in. With the incoming tide came a big skate that swam up out of the deep water looking for something to eat. He saw Ila's brightly painted toenails. He gave her ankle a good bump, as he tried to get that toenail. "Eeeeek! Eeeeeek!" Ila screeched, as she took great leaps toward shore. Tootsie and Allen followed apprehensively wondering what she'd seen. It was triangle in shape, at least three foot from fin tip to fin tip with a little bony tail curled over its gray back.   At high tide they built a house among the drifted logs with wood beams that had floated in.   Sometimes it was a grocery store.   It was stocked with milk bottles, cans, cartons—anything that floated up on the beach.   Pretty pieces of sea washed glass, shells or rocks were legal tender.

Ila with Sharon doll.
Bernice with Shirley Temple doll.

Tootsie and Ila were often accompanied by their dolls, Allen his teddy bear.   The bear was forgotten one day never to be seen again. Did the tide take it away?   Jens occasionally joined the threesome, although he usually felt too old for cowboys and Indians games. Today he led them past his house, past the paint shop's open door.

The keepers were busy sharpening tools on the emery horse and preparing paint for the annual paint jobs.   The children went quietly past giving the open door a large berth, for parents could always think of jobs to do.   Across the tramway they went, and up the brush covered bank to high ground.   Ah, here was Pedersen's barn.

Once they reached a smooth trail, they could clippety clop as horses do, on to Jens' hideout.   They were on the cliff overlooking the apple house, both homes, Puget Sound and magnificent Mt. Rainier.

A set of wooden stairs allowed passage to the houses below. Off to the left, through huckleberry and salal brush in a little dip was the hideaway. The floor, side and roof were made of reed mats that had washed ashore from strange distant lands. The room barely held four kids squeezed in. A candle flickered inside a tuna can. Everyone was sworn to secrecy as each one tried to smoke a salal leaf. The hut soon filled with smoke, so the party broke up. Jens disappeared. The others headed down the long flight of stairs, as they bragged about who was going to have the most butter and peanut butter spread on their homemade bread.

Deep into fall, a couple of men from Redondo Beach came over to the beaches near the lighthouse to collect logs to barge home for firewood. Wyman kept an eye on them for there was a considerable chop building off the point. About 4 o'clock they headed back across the sound with their load. They had an outboard, but it was no match for the tides, wind and currents they had to face out there in the middle. They should have cut the lines to their load of wood, but they didn't think of it soon enough. We could hear them calling for help as they clung to the edge of the swamped skiff.

Wyman and Pete ran to the boat house, and dragged the largest boat out to the water. They threw blankets and thermoses of coffee into the 15 foot row boat, and rowed out to save the men if they could. They brought in two grateful men. They sat by the wood cook stove with feet in buckets of warm water sipping hot coffee. Their boat was lost. Father loaned them each one of his union suit underwear to go home with and much to his regret, for they never returned them.

During winter storms, ponds of sea water built up in the basement. The sump pump got clogged up or just burned out, so the sea filled the whole basement with about two feet of water. What a pool for boat launching! There were wooden platforms used to keep wood, coal and other storage up off the floor about four inches. An empty one made a good raft.

Allen made sailboats from walnut shells filled with paraffin, and a toothpick for a mast. The sail was a three cornered piece of paper. He had a whole fleet.

Elementary school was at Docton. There were two rooms dividing the grades from one through four, and five through eight. Mrs. Ryder taught grades one through four, while Mr. Ryder taught grades five through eight. The whole school had band uniforms, so once a week we practiced with Mrs. Ryder as she played the piano. The school children used sleigh bells, handled belles, tambourines, flutes, xylophone, spoons, castanets and so on. A photographer took our picture, when we were dressed in the nice white and red uniforms. Someone thought Ila's light green bows on her pigtails would clash with the white uniforms. So Ila's light green bows were pulled back. In the picture Ila looked very pouty, because she liked her pigtails and bows, and wanted them to show.

Dockton School (September 1939)

Mrs. Keene was a widow friend of Ruth's who lived in Docton. She invited Ila to have lunches with her that winter. She made nice warm chocolate to go with their sandwiches. It was an unforgettable treat. Ruth took Mrs. Keene to Vashon to shop late one afternoon.

By evening time a very heavy fog settled down. They were creeping along guiding the car by the yellow center line and the gravel along the shoulder, which frequently disappeared in the heavy mist. Suddenly the lights of an oncoming car filled their lane. Ruth turned off onto the shoulder hitting the beginning post of a road guard dead center. The other car stopped, and the driver went over to ascertain damages. He was nice, owned a restaurant in Seattle, and carried insurance. Aside from the damage done to the front of the car, Mrs. Keene was the only one hurt. She had hit the windshield, cracking it. She got a goose egg on her forehead and of course, whiplash. The case settled out of court. Ruth got the amount of money necessary to repair the damage to the car, plus enough for a new dress. Mrs. Keene got enough to salt away for a rainy day.

Later, Mrs. Keene's house was the sight of a Bible study that Wyman had with some of Allen's and Ila's friends. Afterward their friends invited them to a catechism class at Docton's Catholic Church. Dad thought it a courtesy to let them attend. They survived! They never dared tell their friends how frightened they were. They expected the walls of that church to open up and envelop them, or that lady in the black habit might snatch them away, hiding them in her billowing skirt.

At Christmas the classes exchanged gifts, which were opened after the play was over. The whole school put on a play of bunnies, sunbeams and owls—everyone having to memorize parts. The costumes were made of flannel and crepe paper made by the students' mothers.

Sunbeam (Ila), orange and yellow crepe paper for Christmas school play 1939.

Some mothers made extra costumes for the children who couldn't afford them, or else the teacher found something left from previous years.

School days seldom went past May 30th. The berry fields had to be plowed and weeded. All too soon berry season started with whole families turning out to the fields and orchards. Mothers and children picked for their favorite farmer. Ruth liked to pick for the very small farmer, where she and the girls were the only ones in the field.

First, there were pretty pink currents, gooseberries, youngberries, boysenberries, pie cherries. Then we went on to another farm to finish the season in strawberries. Allen picked so slowly, by day's end the berries were so compacted that the carrier still needed to be filled to look full. Ellen suffered in the sun. Her idea of making money lay in a proper education that would lead to a job behind the keys of a typewriter. She made a few dollars for school clothes picking berries even so. Lavinia did quite well. Ruth was pleased with her $20.00. Ila made about $5.00 that season.

Early on, the Burtons joined us for Watchtower study on Sundays. The keepers alternated Sundays off, so Wyman and brother Burton would alternate the meeting place—the Burton's place or ours.

Their son, Merle, had built his own single engine airplane. Wyman paid him for some fuel for his plane in exchange for a ride. Merle landed his little plane on the beach at low tide right in front of the station. He made several takeoffs and landings getting each member of the family in the air. Allen and Ila sat together in the same seat for their trip. It was so thrilling! But it was just too, too, short though. There below, Vashon Island lay, surrounded by sky blue water with the fields in various states of cultivation, looking like a beautiful patchwork quilt.

Pods of Orca would play right in front of the house. Whoever saw them first would alert everyone by calling, "The black fish are coming! The black fish are coming!" They put on a theatrical display just for us, jumping, diving over each other, slapping their huge tails, making sprays like fountains going, "Spisssh!" as they expelled water from their spouts. Sometimes they played off the point. One young whale misjudged when taking a flying leap over the shoal that divided the deep water at the end of the point. It landed on top, water so shallow it was unable to wiggle off. Wyman was greatly concerned. He didn't want it to die there for the tide was going out. He ran to get Pete to help push this mammoth off the shoal with long two by fours. They had no way of knowing if it would turn on them. They ordered everyone to stay well up out of the way in the driftwood. They each took a position toward the center of the huge fish and gently with increasing pressure pushed against its great side ever wary of that huge tail and its sharp teeth that seemed so close. Their effort was successfully rewarded as its carcass began to float. With a flip and a twist it dove into the deep side of the shoal never showing itself again to its rescuers.

The keepers were not trained in life saving. Neither could they swim. Their parts in saving lives were dictated mainly by conscience and presence. By habit they watched the weather and the goings on the sea. A winter storm was brewing as they watched a Foss Tug pulling a heavy raft of logs into the northern currents of the point. The tug swamped so quickly there wasn't time for any safety measures. The crew's very first cries for help were heard by Wyman and Pete who threw blankets into the row boat, unhesitatingly heading to the rescue.

Ruth watched some of the trip through a three foot telescope dad owned. Once the men were in the boats, she went inside to make a fresh pot of coffee and to stoke the fire. She prepared a couple of warm wool blankets, hot water bottles, buckets of warm water for the men's feet. They arrived with clenched teeth and uncontrollable shivers. The Foss Tug Company remembered the keepers each Christmas thereafter with a five pound box of Almond Roca. It was evenly divided and shared between the two families.

Ila was to be Queen of the North in this year's Christmas play. Mrs. Ryder thought that with her long hair combed out from the pigtails it would look like the zig zags of lightening in addition to the crown of zig zagged tinsel. The white crepe paper gown reached the floor with zig zags of tinsel on each tier.

On the day of the play, when one final practice session was scheduled, Ila came down with a fever, and was kept home from school. Mrs. Ryder supposed Ila was out of the play, so she shortened the script, and drilled Olga for the part. Ruth thought Ila had improved some, so she brought her to school for the evening play anyway. Her pink cheeks needed no rouge.

The following year, Ellen and Lavinia made enough berry picking money to pay their way on an old rehabilitated school bus that was to take a group of Christians to the St. Louis, Missouri, "Children of the King" convention. The bus was haywired together and broke down occasionally, but mere faith and determination made that old bus do the round trip. Mostly, they slept in hay stacks along the road; and they made their own lunches as they went along. Ellen got heat stroke at the convention, and had to spend most of it at First Aid under a shady tarp sipping salt water. That was not her kind of weather.

Lavinia survived just fine. They both received a pretty blue book with the name "Children" written in gold letters on its cover. Everyone stayed in high spirits not complaining—just having a good time as they returned home on the old bus.

The inland waters of Puget Sound are often considered the banana belt, because it seldom retains winter's snow. Children deplore the fact that they can never find enough to make a snow ball much less a snowman. By New Year all the children would wish to be living in snow country. The winter was about to perpetuate this same weather pattern, when late in February the skies dumped three foot of glorious snow on the area. It hung on for more than a few days, so most everyone had to make at least one trek to the grocery store on foot.

Wyman invited Pederson to go first, then the next day Wyman went. The nearest grocery was at Portage—about five miles from Robinson Point. In pioneer days, supplies had to be portaged across the inlet. Now the marsh had been filled with good solid earth and rock from the quarry. This connected Maury Island (Robinson Point is on Maury Island) and Vashon Island by land, so the two are considered as one. The skies seemed gray and threatening, but the trip proved successful in obtaining the necessary supplies.

Someone decided schools were to be consolidated—doing away with one and two room school houses. A couple of the older girls, Goldie and Olga, came to Ila and asked, "Would you like to plan, and arrange the final good-bye party?" "What is that?" asked Ila. Goldie and Olga explained: "Every year one of the students plans a going away party and keeps it secret from the teachers. All of the students are involved. You collect contributions from everybody to pay the $5.00 rental of the community hall and another contribution collection for the teacher's presents. We will help you." "Okay, I'd like to do it," responded Ila enthusiastically. Ila was delighted to have been asked to hold such a responsible job in honoring the teachers. Until now she had not quite comprehended the impact the consolidation was having on a past way of life. Probably for Mr. and Mrs. Ryder, it would be the end of their teaching careers. They wouldn't be teaching at Burton next year. There were punch and cookies and streamers, paper covered tables and ice cream. The Ryders expressed surprise. Mrs. Ryder played the piano, while the children scrambled among musical chairs. Mr. and Mrs. Ryder were presented with their gift from all the students. Then they were bid, "Good-bye! Good-bye!"

Wyman had been cleaning brass, checking fuel levels on the generators, and sweeping up in the lighthouse tower. He sat down for a quick rest, and switched on the radio. The announcer was talking like an auctioneer. Something big had just broke, yes, the Japanese had bombed Pearl Harbor! The American navy was nearly destroyed. He listened to the rest of the details to make sure it wasn't some mistake. He ran to the house to tell Ruth. As he turned to climb the stairs to the kitchen, he came face to face with Ila. "The Japanese have bombed Pearl Harbor!" he exclaimed, and as if to impress her more profoundly, he repeated the statement. "What is Pearl Harbor?" the eleven year old asked in amazement to see her father in such a state of anxiety. Pearl Harbor came to mean war news every morning before leaving for school. Pearl Harbor also came to mean buying war bonds or stamps to fill a book for a bond. In addition, it came to mean patriotic songs—sad songs of young people in love, who might forever be parted. Furthermore, it came to mean movies of underground heroes or aviators downed in enemy territory. And sadly, it came to mean the gruesome tales of the incarceration and incineration of Jews and Jehovah's Witnesses.

These were days of rationing with stamps, buttons and coupons for sugar, butter, tires and gas. Ruth warned the children, "Never talk to strangers. Never mention anything about the affairs at the lighthouse. Don't talk to other children about anything military." The radio said about the same thing in other words, so we obeyed implicitly. The war was never discussed at school. It simply hung like a black cloud over everything.

The Albee children's religion made them targets of insults. The most demeaning and insulting was when someone threw a "heil Hitler" salute at them. In Germany, Witness children would not "heil Hitler" or "heil" its flag either. The parents were put in concentration camps, and the children were given to foster families. Witness children had been taught that to salute the flag was the same as bowing to an image. A Christian didn't do it. The Supreme Court at the beginning of the war established compulsory flag salute for the nation. Later, they reversed the decision just as the school board had a meeting to discuss expelling Ellen and Lavinia from school for non-salute. The meeting wasn't canceled so Wyman, Ruth and a minister representing the Watchtower Society presented the recent position of the U. S. Supreme Court to the Board. The Board acquiesced, but everyone thought it best if the girls stayed out of school for a year, while emotions cooled off. Ellen and Lavinia went looking for jobs.

The government letters to Wyman began to be addressed to "The Commanding Officer of Robinson Point Light Station, Sir." Having only a fifth grade education, Wyman never felt entitled to any superior recognition. The title amused him. In due time, Uncle Sam turned the Lighthouse Service over to the Coast Guard. Those keepers who wished to join the Coast Guard could, others would be assigned Civil Service Positions.

Young Coast Guardsmen began to be assigned to various lighthouse stations. Our first Coast Guardsman was Manni, from some inland state. The lighthouse children were amused that the government would send someone from such a land locked state to protect our shores from the ocean going invader. He had good manners, shared dinner at the family table, and laughed and joked with Ellen and Lavinia and their friends who came to visit from Seattle. Ruth thought the girls kept him in his proper place when (Margaret? Bev?) dedicated the popular song "Scatterbrain" to him and by playing a couple choruses on the piano.

Allen had tied a rope to a small raft that was floating by one day, and anchored it to some immovable driftwood. It was made of three logs with one by fours nailed across to form a floating platform. Manni would dive off it at high tide, and swim with powerful strokes out to the shipping lanes, then back. By summer's end, Jens, Tootsie, Allen and Ila had learned to dive just from watching him. He helped cut wood from the beach for the residential furnaces, learned how to operate the auxiliary engines—gas and diesel, and did the usual painting maintenance, and shared watch.

Then there was Bill from Colorado. He was blond, tall, six foot, blue eyed and very well mannered. It doesn't seem he was with us very long. When he left, the government sent groups of men who stayed in tents pitched between the residences and the lighthouse.

Ruth was close to being six months along in her fifth pregnancy. No one had noticed yet. She thought it time to start letting it be known. She started with her older friends who must have thought she needed their advice. "Get an abortion," they declared. "Anyone your age shouldn't have to start raising kids again." It was Ruth's turn to be shocked. Ellen and Lavinia condemned her for bringing added expense upon the family, since mother could never find money for school clothes, only home sewn cotton dresses. She gave herself time to settle with these rebuffs before trying the news on Ila.

"Ellen and Lavinia think I'm terrible for this: you're going to have a baby brother or sister in June. How do you feel about it?" "I think it's wonderful!" she exclaimed, absolutely delighted to think of having a real baby to hold, and to play with. Her sisters' attitudes puzzled her. Ila didn't think the situation could be reversed, and the way Ruth's spirits were lifted, others should have entered the spirit of joy to encourage her.

The island doctor had just started requiring his pregnant patients to deliver at his office. "Not me," Ruth declared. Ruth told the doctor, "If you refuse to come, I'll deliver it myself." She would have, too, because she had prepared Wyman to do the delivery, and Lavinia to take the baby, and do the necessary things for it. For a girl who lived in the imaginary world of Saturday Evening Post's love stories of the "tall, dark, handsome" heroes of the day, and asking mother what to do when a boy at school would say, "Hello," Lavinia certainly was not ready for the realities of a tiny new baby. She kept telling mother she couldn't do it, but Ruth's mind was made up. When the doctor *did* come much to everyone's relief, the family was presented with baby boy, Leland.

Leland (6 months old—1942)

Strange objects began washing in upon the beach. The children were warned never to touch them, but to show them to father if it looked like a bomb. He would place it in the paint house for inspection by the government. It had to be identified as American or foreign, active or dud.

Finally Wyman's papers were filled out for transfer to Pier 91 in Seattle. His title there was Machinist's Helper. The machines that arrived were the fine old auxiliary engines from the lighthouses that the young Coast Guardsmen were desecrating. Some were the very engines he had cared for on the stations. He was assigned to repair them, putting them back into working order. He thought it odd that no one else ever worked on them. Do you suppose, kerosene, diesel and gas generators were a thing of the past?

He and Ruth had to look for the first home they had ever owned privately. They chose a home outside Seattle's city limits, which was accessible to Inter Bay where he worked. Their down payment consisted of dad's diamond cluster ring and a couple of Ruth's rings. Having to meet monthly mortgage payments, heating bills, telephone, taxes, electricity became a difficult experience.

Ila was allowed to stay with a girl friend who lived in Burton to finish the two weeks of school and share in the eighth grade graduation exercises. Helen was an exciting, thrilling, adventurous young lady. When in shorts or slacks, you had to tie your shirt tails in a neat granny knot just below the breast making a nice triangle of bare skin just above the waist. Then you went wandering around Burton, looking for boys—ice cream cones, candy bars, happenings—boys. "You always let any boy kiss you," Helen told Ila. "Any boy?" asked Ila. "Sure!" replied Helen. "What if its El Jerko?" asked Ila, "I don't like him," Ila clarified. "Let him kiss you. How else can you have any fun?" replied Helen.

Wednesday night was "Boy Scout meeting" night at Burton. The fellows who belonged to the Scouts who lived in Docton had rowed across the bay to get there. It let out at 7:30 and the girls were on hand to walk with them on the beach. Helen paired off with a Docton boy—El Jerko fulfilled Ila's worst fears.

Nevertheless, you ought to be nice even if he wasn't a replica of Van Johnson. He sidled over to walk with her. After a few steps he took her hand. The others had disappeared behind some huge log. "Are you going to be in Burton long?" he asked. "'Till graduation," Ila answered, tight and frustrated from the uncertainties of her friends advice. "Will you be at graduation?" she asked. "Yeah," he answered. He stopped suddenly, pulled her to him, and smacked her right on the mouth. Frustrated and anxious she broke away and went bumbling down the beach. The next day at school, everyone seemed to know she'd been kissed. She wasn't pleased with this kind of notoriety. Ila was glad to be moving to a new school. It would be easier to choose friends who didn't create impossible situations.

Burton Elementary (June 1944)

Everyone had new dresses for the 8th grade graduation. Anticipation wove a veil of mystery around the occasion, hope that some profound happening would reveal the future pathways of each student. In reality it was the usual formal acceptance of the certificate, well chaperoned, with some socializing over cookies and punch. No one realized the mists of time were closing off the well defined era of the Children of the Lighthouse.

Chapter VI

Seven Devils

Aunt Luella and uncle Ed lived up the Seven Devils Road, about three miles. It starts up a hill out of Charleston, and winds its way along the inland coast to Bandon. One barely gets starting up this hill, and one comes to a "Y" in the road. The left "Y," takes one to Cape Argo Lighthouse, and the right "Y" leads to Shore Acres Park, which originally housed the lumber magnate, Mr. Simpson, at his estate and mansion.

The Seven Devils was an old logging road built of two-by-twelves laid side by side over railroad ties. You always drove carefully, for in those days you had to get yourself undug. There were no service stations for miles. Uncle Ed might bring Midget, the plow pony, to help pull. Also, cars didn't weigh as much at that time. So two or three sprightly men may extricate it with a female steering the wheels back onto the tracks.

Across from the "Y" was Charleston's elementary school where the Metcalf boys—Ted and Lewis—attended. In the mid thirties a little one room school was built about a mile and a half up Seven Devils, where Ted's boys, Donald and Dewey, went in the late thirties and early forties.

Those two kids lived with Luella and Ed as a result of Ted's divorce. Ed, Ted and Lewis were log truck drivers. And since they had some native American blood running in their veins, they would be the first to be laid off, when log cutting was slow, or when log cutting stopped for ice and snow in winter or for fire danger in summer.

Luella kept the ranch running. She herded cows. She fed chickens, a pig, dogs and cats, etc. At milk time, if the cows had not come home, she had to go looking for them. Usually they were across the road down in a gully. On the way, she would call, "Come Boss, come Boss, come Princess, come Beauty!" And Spot would follow the sound of tinkling bells, which hung around the cows' necks. He would round them up, nipping at their heels, guiding them up the side of the ravine.

Back on top, they entered the gate to the fenced-in lane that leads to the barn on the right, with the smoke house off to the left. Whoever was milking that night, placed hay—or grain when they could afford it—in the manger. Then he (or she) sat on the milk stool with a three gallon bucket between his knees to milk. The dog got a large sardine can of milk for his good deed.

The cats sat in a semicircle to receive squirts of milk straight from the cow. A little milk on their fur didn't matter. The cows were confined to the barn and yard for the night. The milk was carried to the house strained through a loose weaved cloth, and poured into shallow pans for the cream to rise. When cream was needed, it was scooped off the top with as little milk as possible for coffee or whatever. The longer it sat, the thicker the cream became, until it all soured. Sour cream was saved for butter along with the rest, but the pig got most of the sour milk.

You entered the house into a congested hallway. Straight ahead on the right was a kitchen hutch, which held the baking needs— spices, cream of tarter, working yeast starter for bread. Underneath the hutch were two bins that tipped out, containing from 50 to 100 pounds of flour or sugar. This area greeted every visitor with the aroma of home baked bread.

This hallway was a narrow passage way that had coat hooks all along the walls to the right and left of the door for everyone to hang their coats and hats on. On the floor were boots, shoes and slippers for every occasion. Straight ahead was a window. The upper half of this window was leaded glass, which drew the sunlight into the hall in rainbow colors. Level with the window was a bench that held Luella's prize house plants, especially the Thanksgiving cactus and the Christmas cactus, both of which bloomed lavishly at their appointed times.

To the right was the kitchen. A crow footed bathtub sat in the corner as you entered. It collected clothes and dirty wash items until they were cleaned and ironed. A 100 pounds sack of potatoes rested there also, handy for peeling and preparing for dinner. The tub was emptied once a week for baths. The cook stove produced plenty of heat. Hot pans of water sat on the stove to warm the cold well water that was emptied into the tub. Kids took turns first—then ladies, then men—all in the same water. If anyone bucked, he was free to carry the used water out away from the house, and carry in fresh water from the well, which was positioned about 10 feet in front of the kitchen stairs.

Layered bricks encircled the top of the well from ground level to about three feet up. A bucket hung from a wheel that lowered it into the well. You had to jerk the rope around until the bucket tipped over. As it sunk, it filled with water. When you brought it up, it was poured into another bucket to carry into the house. Hot water from the stove was added from time to time.

As day would dawn, the roosters would commence crowing, which would not first wake up the household, rather all the denizens of the forest. Sleeping under the attic rafters in a billowy featherbed to be awakened by the robins trill, borders on exquisite delight. The closest match today is for those who tent, or hikers who sleep in bags under the stars. The other birds were doing their twitter, tweets too, but the robin's call seems to echo through the woods, and play on your heart strings as they announced the sun's rising to the whole world.

The old homestead was surrounded by miles of alderwoods, huckleberry, salal. In the deep woods were the Douglas firs. They were known to harbor deer, elk, bear, wild cat, civet cat, skunk, even wild hogs. If these critters were not enough to keep a child from wandering to far from the house, there were cougar, mountain lions or panthers, which treaded these woodland paths silently, stealthily searching for food, a mate or home.

Folklore had it that Bee Taylor walked these paths one night with a kerosene lamp. Suddenly, his fingers touched the soft back of a cougar, which had joined him for a slight safari. It left him as silently as it arrived. Poor Bee forced himself to keep cool, keeping a steady pace until the cougar turned aside. Then he broke all time records getting to Ed's place.

When she was a child of about four, Luella's youngest sister, Ruth, ran away down these paths getting lost. The family dog, Bounder, stayed with her into the night. It is said that Bounder saved her life, for she was about a mile from home. The dog's bark lead them to her.

This describes the wild country these folks came from who decided to go to California to care for Daisy, who had contracted tuberculosis.

Grandma and grandpa Powell lived up the Seven Devils also. They arrived here at Seven Devils by covered wagon about 1897. They came from farm country in Minnesota. Harmon (grandpa) opened a little grocery store in Charleston. When too many people were unable to pay for the groceries, they charged. Grandpa sold the store, and headed for California at grandma's pleading. The letters they wrote to their daughter and family tell the rest of the story.

Chapter VII

Tribulation 1925-30

Wedding picture of Thomas & Ruth Albee – 1915

Red Bluff, California
September 14, 1925

Dear Ruth & Wyman,

(In the morning)
We are having a good time. We are going to eat dinner at Red Bluff, if we can get there. We have from three to six flat tires a day. Fay's trailer broke down yesterday, one wheel broke up, trailer turned over and only two fruit jars broke one tomatoe/wild blackberries.

All are well. Momma and Papa are standing the trip fine and you should see the travelers or tourists. Also the Siskiyous Mtn. some high precipices of some distances Gee!

We got in a thunder storm and pour down proper the 3rd day from home. Bedding is all wet yet some of it got soaked didn't last long, but while it did it meant business. It was about twelve miles from Weed where we were the closest to Mt. Shasta.

We are waiting for Fay, I guess he has a flat tire poor devil. We can't turn around with our trailer and I guess he will come soon. It is hotter than I like sitting still.

I can't say I am very fond of this country yet.

The most mileage a day has been 71 miles. We have flat tires, flat tires first one then the other we had all the trouble first and now poor Fay he's having his but we are expecting our turn any minute. We had two flat tires yesterday, first one just a mile from where we camped. Then in the afternoon Fay's trailer turned over and that ended that days journey.

September 13, Sunday:
Ted is reading traffic laws in California, now.

We are all enjoying ourselves outside of those trifles.

We registered our cars in Redding.

We are camped for dinner just out of Red Bluff. River water contaminated, can't use for cooking or any purpose. Backhouse or toilets screened tighter than the dickins to keep flies from spreading germs. "I like Coos best."

Mama is played out "sleepy."
Well this all from us today.
Hope you are fine and well.
They hold you up here, coffee Hill Bros. coffee 65¢, other 67¢ a lb.
I guess this is enough of my gab so good-bye.

Luella

Pasadena Calif.
3019 East colo. St.

Dear Ruth & Family   October 10, 1925

I wrote to you once before, but I want to write to you tonight so will try. I don't know hardly what I will write about only to tell you how we are and what we are doing. We are all feeling pretty well, but we are all whining about the living. We are living harder up than we ever did in our lives. Trying to save money to pay on a place to live in. If we could only get located so we could get to doing something to bring in something, instead of paying out all the time.

Opal got a job on the linotype in a little town called Elsinore, about 80 miles from here. She thought she would get along all right, and Fay got a job the next morning after they went over, for $4.50 per day. But they didn't want to take Harmon out of school till they was sure they would like it and stay. So they left Harmon with us this week. So Daisy and I have had the two boys on our hands this week. But all things on this earth come to an end and so has this week. We look for Fay and Opal over here in the morning and then if all is well I suppose they will take Harmon over to Elsinore to go to school.

It has rained only two days since we came here and I guess it is going to rain tonight. It rained on the 3rd and some on the fourth. And it has been cooler ever since it rained. We are all sitting around tonight in the house without a fire perfectly comfortable, except Papa, he lays around on the bed all day long shivering with the cold and wondering why we don't get any news from the kids.

Money is getting low and we will surely starve, etc. We like it first rate, but if we only could get a little home so we could raise a garden and have something to think about I think we would like it better. We have the offer of a little place now for a couple hundred down and 25 dollars per month till paid. If the kids at home would help us what they could with the down payment I think we could make the payments then.

I think Daisy is a whole lot better now than when we landed here. She coughs some yet but she is stronger I know, but here in the camp is not the right place for her.

I must tell you about the town where Opal is. It is a little town up in the mountains on the shore of a lake about 5 miles long and about two miles wide, there is pelicans there and lots of ducks there too. A man came in with 25 ducks while we were there. There is hot spring somewhere near the town, and the water in the faucets is warm enough to wash dishes in. And it tastes of sulphur so strong that it spoiled the coffee for us and the sulphur taste was on everything we cooked.

Now when you write tell us the news. Tell us what they done with the man Metcalf. Did anyone rent the old store yet? Did Frank Wyman take Daisy's cow? Do you ever see Linda? How do you like the new side of the house? etc.

Luella wrote us that the babies was sick. If their bowels are loose get them ripe tomatoes to eat. Give them all they will eat.

We have not seen any of the Bible students yet. We have been cramped in such a little place and we had everything dirty and we did not feel able to send it to the laundry, so I have done it myself. I did not have anything to work with and it took a long time. We have just got caught up and Monday is washing day again. I don't suppose we will find out much about them yet awhile.

Well Goodby and write soon. God bless you and keep you.

From your loving Mother Minnie Powell

Pasadena Calif. 3019 East Colo. St.

Cornola
Ethanae P.O.
Riverside
Calif.
Dear Ruth,   11-20-1925

I was going to write to Sister Johnson tonight and as I wrote you only a few days ago this will probably be kind of a short letter. But we received your letter and check enclosed and thought I had better acknowledge receipt of the same and save any wondering or worry whether we got it or not. And I will also answer some of your questions, you asked some time ago whether we got the letter with your other check in it? We did, and we got the letter with Mrs. Herman's letter and Sister Dunson's letter in it. Daisy wrote to Mrs. Herman and got a reply tonight. She writes a kind of lonely letter. Elif. is down to the creek spearing salmon most of the time. So it naturally follows that she is at the house alone. Nobody to sit straddle of her neck, and make her make crooked marks and twisted letters when she tries to write.

Well the more we see of this life the more we thank God for the understanding we have that this evil reign is moving fast and the rule of Christ is coming in so fast, when everyone will understand His Word and His ways and when every creature will not only be happy but will be giving praise and adoration to Him that sitteth on the throne. When we think of these things do we not long for that blessed time. We have not had the privelege of attending class since we left home. We have only run onto one couple and then only for a moment.

We are homesick to see some of the dear ones. We are homesick for the kids and we have had quite a time roughing it too, but we are quite comfortable now and Daisy is just where she should be everybody tells us, so we are just where we ought to be. And maybe the Lord has something for us to do here.

When I say homesick I don't mean we are sitting around with long face and so on, but we wish we could see you all. We wonder if Lavinia can talk much yet. We wonder if Ellen talks plainer yet. We wonder if Lenore is growing taller. If Bryce is the same old sport. We would like to have them all here in a band once more. But we know the Lord will rule and override all things for good for those who love Him and look for His appearing.

I was wondering whether I had written you about *our house*. We moved on the lot on the 11th of Nov. We had a load of lumber come the same day. But there was no carpenters but Papa and Daisy. But they worked at it the best they could and by Sunday they had the foundation laid and the frame work cut out and Sunday Fay and Opal came and brought Doe and another old fellow and they pitched in and put up the frame and put on the sheeting on the roof and some of the side boards. Papa and Daisy finished it nailed down floor and finished siding. The siding is board up and down. The house is 11 X 16. We bought a good grade paper roofing and hired a boy who lives next door to put it on. The cracks in the walls are not battered. And probably won't be for awhile. We have enough to pay the payment on the land, finish paying for the lumber and make a good payment on the stove and then live the best we can for awhile.

Oh! I was going to ask if any of them ever heard of Old Brown? Does he still live in North Bend? I suppose Vi's baby had come long ago. Poor kid!

It has been quite cold down here, there was two nights that it froze ice. It was blowing around here that we could plant garden even in Minnesota in the winter, but would not expect it to grow. But I asked our neighbor if her garden was spoiled and she laughed and said it did not hurt her garden a bit. Daisy and I are going to plant some garden. I don't know whether I told you that Daisy unpacked her flowerbox about four days ago and found all but three of her flowers all right. The patridge tail cactus, Mrs. Cole brought down to Daisy was just as fresh as if it had been put in there yesterday. The geraniums all looked lively but had lost their leaves. She set them out doors and they are livening up fine. You asked if we wanted slips of your plants? Yes we do, but as our house is so small, I think it would be better not to send them before March or April.

Well it is getting late and I washed today and am tired and I guess I will close and go to bed. Write again and tell all about the kiddies and tell Ellen, Aunt Daisy and Grandma often wished Lavinia and her could be here for a little while if Momma and Papa couldn't.

Well good night, love to all and God bless and keep you all.

From your loving Mother

Mrs. Minnie Powell

Elsinore, Calif.

Nov. 30, 1925

Dear Ruth:

Poor old sister Daisy is hopelessly sick. She had a hemorrhage? yesterday and was still spitting up blood this morning. We had a doctor over here and he says she must be gotten in out of the tent as later we will have rain and frost and "she must not catch cold." He seemed to think a cold would end it all quick. The blood she coughed up was dark and clotted. Dr. said it had been there a long time and had dripped in slowly. She feels bad she cried last night when I left. I went over today to take the Dr. subscriptions over. Mamma got a subscription for whiskey and is going to give her egg nog if she can hold it down she hasn't eat anything for four days.

Mamma has held out hopes all the time but now she has given up. She said today she had hoped that Daisy would be well thru this winter. If she could last maybe next summer the sun shine and heat would cure her. But I don't know. She hasn't got any hopes to live for and she broods over her troubble and worries about Ma & Pa. And it won't cure her.

Well Ruth I must close as I must write Luella yet tonight. Write Mama as often as you can she is very busy so excuse her if she don't ans. P.D.Q., she feels so bad about Daisy.

Write soon with love,

Opal & Family

Don't fail to send Papa something each month. If ever he needed it he needs it now. I am out of a job. Will do the laundry tomorrow.

Ethanae Calif.
Nov. 30, 1925
7 P.M.

Wyman & Ruth & Kiddies

Will try to write you a line and it will be a sad one at least for me as I have wrote Warren and told him to call you up. I cannot sleep and so will let you know if I can. You and Ruth always come to our relief in previous times and now I will ask you on Daisy's behalf to send me a check by return mail for $50.00 if you can. I will give you credit for it. So you will not be out, but we are broke we were getting along fine and would soon been almost making our own expenses, but no use to tell you for you know sickness is and we get her all we know to get to make her comfortable. I tell you it is a trial I cannot stand it to speak to her. Poor little forsaken little girl. Worked her life away for one that did not deserve it and at her age has to go. The doctor told Opal she did not have a ghost of a show and he told us she would have to stay in bed for a month. And you know what that means now my dear kids. My eyes water, so I cannot see through my glasses, but someone ought to write and Min is all in you know she is up nights. So much to do I have been trying to help her around the house. And just when Opal and Fay were getting on their feet the Printing shop went the same as broke. But we need Opal with car to get to doctor. Her and Fay paid for the doc or going too. They were just about up on their feet and getting ready to send you that $50.00, don't worry about it, they will get and you will get it. They certainly have helped us and would not buy anything until they knew we were all right. Although they want a home here too. I cannot write about it now, but I believe the *Lord* guided us here for some purpose.

They have a big class at Riverside and I will have Opal take me over soon to get acquainted with speakers in case of need we would know what to do. And I now pray for us all as we grant you a good part in our prayers.

God Bless you all.
Please write.

H. Powell

P.S. We will write Warren everyday, so you can get all we could say if we wrote you all. H.P.
Sell that cow if you possibly can even a little less.

Rornola, Ethanae, P.O.
Riverside, Co. Calif.
Dec. 12, 1925

Dear Sister and Brother,

Will try and write you a few lines today and I don't no whether I can write anything very interesting tho. Well, if I get along as fast writing this letter as I have today it will sure be some letter, I started it early this morning and it is almost to dark to see to write now, some speed to that.

Opal and Fay were over today and will be over again tomorrow as it is Sunday. Uncle Lee and Aunt Eliza came in on us last night and gave us quite a surprise. I told Opal today I felt I was the baby of the family again as last Sunday when Fay and Opal came over, Opal brought me a box of popcorn (made me think of the popcorn feasts with you and Wyman up there). Fay gave me a nice pretty red apple, then Mama went to the store and when she came back she had candy and I never was so hungry for anything in my life, but I wouldn't ask them to get it. I told Mama she must of read my mind. Papa went to the store the other day and he came back with candy for me. Then this morning before Aunt Eliza left she brought me in a piece candy, two oranges and two apples. Do you blame me for feeling like I was the baby again. I'd rather it was someone else getting the treats tho and I could be out spading the garden and planting it and help Papa with his rabbit hutches and going here and there finding out about getting some rabbits and chickens, but I can't do it now. I've been in bed two weeks now and I don't know how much longer. Tho I try to soft soap Mama in letting me get up and dress everyday and sit in a chair, but no go I can't work her. I couldn't walk anyhow so I guess I wouldn't go far.

They built a bedroom off from the kitchen for me and they moved me in yesterday. Well I walked from my bed in the tent to Ralph's bed in the kitchen just a few steps with Mama helping me, but when I stepped up for the tent I reached up with my hands and caught hold of the two by fours and pulled myself up. And I told Mama I would have to learn to walk on my hands because they're stronger than my feet and legs are. Uncle Lee took me the rest of the way when my bed was ready. I got a good backache today tho.

Well, are you getting real sick of this lingo? I haven't forgotten how to play pinocle. Tho I haven't played any since coming down here, wouldn't mind playing a game some evening.

Well, Ruth as much as I'd like to see you all, I wouldn't advise you to bring your babies around me. The Doctor here was very pointed on that point and he even ordered us to send Ralph clear out of county away from me, so I wouldn't like to see other tots brought around where there is such a possibility of them contracting it and this Dr. says they are hopeless when they do. Keizer told you and Mama the same thing.

You know Mama and Ralph planted some onions tonight.

Today is Sunday. Opal and Fay are here and I got my hair cut too. The wind is coming up again so suppose it will blow hell out of things again. Everything seems to grow right along tho.

I'm sorry that ornery little banty had to be a rooster, but I can't change his sex any now.

Opal is out of her job and Fay's is most done. Opal thinks she's on track of a job up to Los Gatos and they hate to leave and go so far north again and we hate to see them, but one has to go where there is work if they expect to live, I guess.

Our windstorm subsided and didn't do anything but fill my nose and lungs up with dust which kept me coughing all afternoon. The little Star plant didn't die after all. It was so dry when I looked at them in Pasadena, I thought it would never sprout and grow, but I put it in a can of dirt and when I took it out of the box over here it had two shoots on it about three inches long so Mama and I were some surprised and tickled too.

I wrote to Luella and Ed to find out how much it would cost to ship Wildy down here and how much red tape there would be to it. If it didn't cost to much we were thinking of having her shipped. Cows means money down here and then you may not get what you call a cow in the bargain. We pay fifteen cents a quart for milk here and you can't see a drop of cream on it either.

Well, I must close there is nothing more to write. If I had my little band of cows here to sold, I wouldn't needed to sold a one under the hundred mark, but such is life, that little if is always in the way.

Here's wishing you all a Merry Xmas and Happy New Year.

With love to all and all write.

Your sister,
Daisy

Ethanae, Calif.
Dec. 27, 1925

Dear Aunt and uncle and Cousins

Tell Ellen and lavinia I got their cards and presents and thanks very much. I think those pictures are just fine so I can remember the light house.

We got more rabbits, got one for Christmas and I got a knife too.

We have had quite a time Christmas day and day after for it was so hot we almost cooked, but today was not so hot.

Well I have to start school tomorrow.

I spent a week at Lake Elsinore and it is a beautiful place especially from the hill top. I may get a picture and if I do I will send you one.

I just got through making a large airplane and it is going to be a dandy too. I'll ware my new knife Grandpa and Grandma gave me out.

Your nephew
Ralph Taylor

Ralph has a $10.00 Ford. He took the folks home in it Monday, but he hasn't a driver's license yet.

O.E. [Opal Elliott]

Ethanae, Calif.
April 22, 1926

To Wyman & Ruth & Ellen & Lavinia,

Come and see me again we read your letter with check enclosed thanks. We thought you forgot us but glad to get it we are in terrible circumtances but the Lord willing we have to pull out in time. I tell you we have found Loyal Friends even in Calif. that has helped us along and took our word for pay. Your check today went on our rent. We are still $50.00 behind. The winter here is like every place dull, but we have no cause to worry for this will be the richest harvest for 40 years, so they say, and all are rejoicing. The rain did 2 or 3 inches above the average fall. We have about 400 rabbits in all but will not make anything from them till fall. As we expect to breed 300 does about 1st left as 3 months of the hottest weather we cannot breed. Fay and Opal bought them and are furnishing the feed. One bale hay don't last only 3 feeds or 1½ day and hay 30 dollars per ton it is coming down. Now $10.00 in field loose but we cannot handle it loose yet. No sooner when our 300 litters they average about 8 to doe we kill all over that mostly.

Our garden is fine. Peas just beginning to bloom, water mellons all up, potatoes almost to eat. Tomatoe plant are fine, will set out more. I have the ground all ready and watered. Spuash is good and all the garden is fine. We plan on tomatoes, mellons, beans and spuds in plenty when you come down.

You all seem to think will take a fortune to come down here, but it won't. You can drive here in 5 days easy and we don't think is anything. Luella and the kids can tell you if they will and you can see quite a site if you're here when our 300 does litter. About 2400 rabbits over $1000.00 worth at 8 to 10 weeks old then we will get on our feet again. Keep this quiet. And now my pen is dry.

To balance you after now is $36.66 if you can send $25.00, 1st May if you can. The other I want you to pay McDaniels I owe for last ad when Brother Baker spoke and I want that paid. Will send you the bill next month.

Pray for us and write often.

H. Powell

Ethanae, Calif.
July 24th '26

Dear Sister & Brother,

Will try to write you a letter now in answer to one which arrived quite a while ago, but have been busy and sick and visiting so did not get around to write before so you'll have to excuse me, cause I do the best I can. I suppose you have heard all about our *wonderful hot place* by now? Really and truly what did they think of it down here? Everybody has been sick since they left with summer flue, papa tried hard to croak with it but couldn't. Ralph was sick a couple of days and Maw, well she works right along but looks darned bad and I got mad and over done to help matters out but I go anyhow most of the time, yesterday I didn't do nothing but lay around, but am trying again today.

Some day when I feel so disgusted I don't know what to do with myself, I'll be on the track when the fast through train comes from Hemet. One is better off anyway, when they can't work and got no money. Got to stay around and watch things. Go behind and see your kid going around with his ass sticking out and no under clothes to wear. Wish that white livered 'Lou Henry' had to go that way. Maybe he pay what he owed a fellow there. Seems to me, if I didn't have any more to look after there he has, I could squeeze out enough to pay for a couple of cheap brooders.

Tomatoes are ripening slowly and the watermelon all ripening at once and are spoiling. They are nice but can't eat them, they come back up the hill. Wish you had some of them, I'll bet the kiddies would like them. How was the cucumbers? Picked a tub full day before yesterday and have one ten gallon keg full of them, put down in dill, will be good when you get here with the wheel barrow.

I planned on getting job as agent for a company and go around taking orders and thought I would hit your country, but since I heard Wyman had it in for all the peddlers and agents and what he wasn't going to do with them, wasn't worth thinking about and so I got scared out and never took the job. *Good night.*

Oh! don't plan on coming to Calif. to settle. If you want to live where Marna is, she has just made up her mind to go to Alaska when we get rich. There it is cool and nice, flowers the year around and so on.

Ta! Today is a genuine scorcher, but the wind is blowing now but it is hot as hell. Marna has got warmed clear through at last and it don't seem so nice as she thought it would. Tell Luella's folks they left to quick to see the best weather, ha, ha. Also tell her that breaking out on Lewi's is called watermelon poisoning and Doc had it last year and Ralph too and had to quit eating watermelons down here and Ralph has got to quit eating them again too.

Well, it is pretty near the end of a perfect day and everybody has been lazy and slept most of the day when they wasn't leaving for Alaska.

Ta. I'm going out after a squash to cook for supper pretty quick and bake spuds. Had roasting ears last night the second mess out of the garden. If we ever get some shade trees around it wouldn't be so bad, but out in the middle of the valley with the sun boiling right down and no shade it is no wonder, it gets hot.

Opal may be down tonight. Fay's work or crew is moving over to El Monty and he goes over today so that will split their house hold again.

The sweat is rolling off me in streams instead of drying up. I can't think of much of anything to write about and everything I could write I suppose you have been told all about it by now too. Have a milk goat and milk her myself, already know that, Luella told me, when she was here ha. Am I right?

Well, I got nine flocks of little rabbits in the nest all come since July seventh. One old rabbit had thirteen little ones. Opal got here and they have supper pretty near ready now and the kids are off on a rampage some where' s in our big city, ha! ha!

Well, they called supper so will close for now and will write some more bull after awhile. Today is Sunday and Mama is over to the hall working. They're all working and Opal, Doc, and Harmon are cleaning the rabbits. Ralph has beat it. Papa the pains to call him everything mean to him he could, so he up and beat it and wouldn't help. God my head aches and I wish I was in hell, I think it would be a dam sight pleasanter anyway. I got some watermelon rind on cooking, getting ready to preserve. I made some already and had good luck with it and also made some plum butter and it was pretty good too. Do you like such stuff? Nothing better than fooling with fruit and vegatables to can? I always liked to can things.

I suppose Luella has told you what the last Dr. said that looked me over while they was here and all about what he said about curing me and soon. Well, I wish I could try his treatments and see if there is anything to it.

Well, I will have to close as I can think of nothing more to write and I want to get outside, pull Beauty some fresh weeds and give her some fresh water.

So write soon and all the news and would like to have dinner with you and the kiddies.

Love,
Daisy.

Jan. 19th 1927

Dear Ruth & Wyman & little kids,

How do you do? We have waited for an answer from you or anyone from up there except—Luella wrote sometime ago but, she dated her letter 5 & 15th of Jan. 1926 & so I got the laugh on her again for Stale news Ha Ha.

Well, I hope you are all well. Luella stated the kids had been awful sick but, better now & it was cold & wet & stormy but that was the way you like it. Instead of sunny California. Our weather has been good lately but some colder than last year. Have the garden you stated all in we had strawberries, lettuce, and radishes yesterday out of the garden for dinner. Well, here goes with pencil and pen leaked over the paper & my hand & one good stamp & then went dry about 2 times after such a mess as this.

Our roosters are just right to eat & we were going to sell them & of course the price dropped right down & now we eat them. We never see another dime, it beats the duce we cannot get no money & so hard if but Faith can finally bust him come what may. Say, did you see Mrs. Clements and what did she say?

How's babe? I had a dream of him last night & when I woke up the tears had run down my face & under my head till the pillow was all wet & I could not sleep no more. I worry about him. Wish I could see him right now the way I feel I surely think he would get better down here. My leg took a spell yesterday & I could not walk on it. It was just like a hinge go right over no use. It is some better to day. Minnie is getting 5 days a week at the hall if it up keep. She will have a steady job if she can hold it down. She says she is ready to work till she drops. Well you got the old road ok at last from the bridge to Bastundoff that is good & I heard Frank Yonker was a dog killer & I don't blame him a bit either I wish you would eat a big fish for me any kind & write & tell me how it tasted & how I fell after eating it can you do it? Well, write me all the news & tell Ellen & Lavinia I am looking for them to come and see me. Daisy has been gaining, but caught cold & set-back again, but better today.

Good Bye
H. Powell

Romoland, Calif.
Mar. 6th - 27

Dear sister Ruth and all,

I'll try writing you a few lines today tho I feel mighty punk, I couphed nearly all night and this morning I'm sore all over. I've been doing some changing around since I wrote you last.

They have been after me to go to that county hospital ever since last June and everybody said that was just the place for me. So I went but I didn't stay long. They come and got me on a Wednesday and the Monday following Mama come after me and brought me home again. I didn't get enough to eat and I had to wait on myself and they never done a thing for my throat but told me to stay in bed and quit talking Ha! Ha! And I decided if that was all there was to it I might as well be home so I am.

The garden is just fine now but I can't eat the onions or radishes and they look so good too. And Papa has pretty near everything else up and growing. The trunips are pretty near big enough to thin and then will have some good greens.

It is a pretty day, the birds are singing like they were so happy they didn't no what to do. Mamma is working today and Papa is my nurse. There has been some trouble around about kids working and some parents were arrested and fined $150.00 to $250.00 and you know Ralph. He got scared right there and wouldn't work any more until he got a permit. Though have been kind of slow about it, but Mrs. Mobley will have it for him when she comes back Monday so he will go to work again this coming week. Opal said they would be over a while today and I hope they do come. She made mama up a dress by one of her patterns and it looks fine only color then black. The black birds are just thick out this morning.

My R I R hens are just laying to beat the band, Mama got seven eggs yesterday and she says she gets eight every now and then. May 18th will be. I've been coughing so I did not feel like writing and I don't feel much like it now but thought I must finish. Well, I will write a little more, though I don't know what it will be.

There is a new house started on the back lot of our second lot. It has been kind of rainy and today the sun is shining.

Snookiness is curled up a sleep at my feet. Gave a oil and kerosene bath a few days ago for mang caught from where them rabbits was and mama has about made her mind up the goats have got it too. Mama has been putting in flowers and I guess they are all doing fine.

This all and I'm coughing my fool head off every minute or two so by, by, and write.

Your loving sister,
Daisy

Cape Argo Lighthouse
May 19, 1927.

Dear Ruth:

Received too letters today, was glad to get them. Barker was to town yesterday, but did not get any letters. I went over to the Bridge today. Frank Wyman was just leaving for town, so I rode as far as Luella's and waited there till he picked me up he got the mail, my pants is there in post office. I haven't enough money to get them, they come to $11.15 will leave them there till I get my next check. Warren and Luella were pretty tired when they got back, Luella looks all worn out today.

No, I'm not mad because you stayed down, I think you done just right. I would like to be with you but you know how it is with me. If you can come home on stage or train alone as it would cost two much for me to come down, as soon as we can get the money we will go down together this fall, how's that? Get price on stage and train to Roseburg I will meet you there. Train would be the easiest, stage cheeper suit yourself. Glad you are enjoying the sunshine, it has rained and blowd past four days still raining.

May 20. It is fine here this morning sun shine warm. I got a letter from Henry. They have a 6½ lb. girl and doing fine. I'll bet Henry is stepping high now. Will close for this time, write soon.

Wyman

Cape Arago Lighthouse
May 19, 1927.

Dear Ruth:

Received too letters today was glad to get them
Barker was to town yesterday but did not get any letters
I went over to the Bridge today Frank Wyman was just
leaveing for town so rode as far as Luella's and waited
hhere till he picked me up he got the mail, my pants
is there in postoffice I havent enough money to get
them they come to 11.15 will leave them there till I
get
     my next check. Warren and Luella were pretty tired
when they got back, Luella looks all worn out today.

No I'am not mad because you stayed down, I think
you done just right, I would like to be with you but
 you know how it is with me. if you can come home on
stage or train alone as it would cost two much for me
to come down, as soon as we can get the money we will
go down togather this fall, hows that. Get price on
stage and train to Rosegurg I will meet you there.
Train would be the easiest stage cheaper suit your
self. glad you are enjoying the sunshine, it has rained
and blowed past four days still raining.

May 20, it is fine here this morning sun shining warm.

I got a letter from Henry they have a $6\frac{1}{4}$ lb. girl
and doing fine I'll bet Henry is stepping high know.
Will close for this time, write soon.

                    Wyman

Wyman typed most of his letters hunt and peck method. This is an actual copy of his letter.
Also, this is a photocopy of the envelope it was sent in. The yellow color is from aging, and
that's the way the copier picked it up.

May 20, 1927.

Ellen Truth Albee:

Dear Ellen, When are you coming home to Daddy? Don't you know that Daddy is lonesome with out his big girl. Daddy has to eat dinner all alone.

Snowball says cheap, cheap, cheap. Where is Ellen? I want her to come home. Poor little dolly's are lonesome too. No one to play with.

Daddy has got to go to work good-bye.

From Daddy

May 20, 1927.

Lavina Love Albee:

Dear Lavinia, Smokey has got great big wings now and flies all around he thinks he is some chicken. Tell Fay that Smokey can lick his chickens all to pieces.

Poor old Paddy say meow, meow, meow Where is Vinny and Ellen? I want them to come home. Daddy will half to go give Smokey a drink of water and mail this letter.

Good bye from Dad.

May 20, 1927.

Ellen Truth Albee:

Dear Ellen when are you comming home to
Daddy doant you know that Daddy is lonesom with out his big girl, Daddy has to
eat dinner all alone.

Snowball/cheap,cheap,cheap where is
Ellen I want her to come home. Poor little
dollys are lonesom too no one to play with.

Daddy has got to go to work good bye.

From Daddy

Wyman typed most of his letters hunt and peck method. This is an actual copy of his letter.
Also, this is a photocopy of the envelope it was sent in.

May 20, 1927.

Lavania Love Albee:

Dear Lavania Smokey has got great big wings
know and flys all around he thinks he is
some chicken. Tell Fay that Smokey can
lick his chickens all to peaces.

Poor old paddy says meow, meow, meow
where is Vinny and Ellen I want them to
come home,Daddy will half to go give Smokey a drink of water and mail this letter.

Good bye from Dad.

Wyman typed most of his letters hunt and peck method. This is an actual copy of his letter.
Also, this is a photocopy of the envelope it was sent in. The yellow color is from aging, and
that's the way the copier picked it up.

Romoland, Calif.
July 1st 1927

Dear Ruth and Wyman:
    Also Dear Ellen and Lavinia:

We have got the days work done for once at 8:30 o'clock, so I thought I would try and write you the going on in this part of the world. The next day after you left.

Warren and family arrived; they sent June and Bob in ahead to see if we would know them. We did. We knew them the minute we set eyes on them. June has grown quite a lot but she looks just the same. Bob is just the same. Poor little kid, crazy to hunt. Warren took him as often as he dared, and he certainly did leave a glorious time killing rabbits.

Grandpa Doc, Ralph Taylor, Harmon Elliott, Fay Elliott sitting on the running board, Grandpa Powell and Grandma Minnie Ellen

One evening, they took Warren's Studebaker and Fay and Warren and Bob and Harmon and Ralph, and Doc went along to see the fun. They killed 15 rabbits and Bob killed 5 and Harmon 3. Papa and I was along that night and we didn't get home till 2 o'clock. Those times was to much for Bob's strength though he did enjoy it so much. We had two or three days that he did not feel a bit good and his test's was bad. They were worried over him and wrote to Barlte about him. But, he got better and was feeling fine day before yesterday when they left. They stayed just two weeks Warren pitched his tent here by the side of Daisy sunbath house and slept in their own bed. Bryce has changed a bit in looks but is a little bigger, and Eleanor is just as cute as she can be. She says and does some of the oddest things, and she is spoiled to a frazzle. Ellen and Lavinia know how it is, don't you? And it is not much wonder is it, Ellen? We would spoil them too wouldn't we?

Myrtle thought the weather was pretty hot, I don't think she liked our country very well. Warren got a job with Fay over in Arizona and Fay will probably start Monday or Tuesday. Warren thought he would go on and do a little exploring while the rest came. They, Opal and Fay, have to move out of that place Sunday. They will move over here and Opal and Harmon will stay here with us for a few weeks before they go. Poor little Harmon had been having a time since you left. As soon as he got over that sick spell so they took his tonsils & adnoids out. They look pretty bad and he had to go the second time and have some trimming done. Aug. 10th 1929.

Well, Dear Ruth. I started this letter the first day of July and this is the 10th of August. Things have happened so fast. I have not had a chance to finish it. Now I will send it? So you can see how things seemed when I started it and see how it is now.

When Warren started for Arizona the last of June because Bobbie wanted to hunt and fish. Fay was supposed to start in a day or two, but their starting was delayed a day or two and a day or two more and then we got word that Bobbie was not feeling very well but not serious though they worried over him as they always did. Then we got word, a telegram that Bobbie was dead. I wish you could have read that telegram. It was the saddest thing I ever read and ended with, "A sad good night, from Warren." Papa said he wrote you all the details. How they took him from Mary's Lake, where he took sick to a little town Winston, I think was the name to a doctor but the doctor did not seem to understand his case and he was in so much pain they thought he would die and they put him in the car and went to Flagstaff a distance of about 70 miles with him screaming with pain all the way. Took him to a hospital where the fool doctor said he had acute apendicitis and rushed him onto the operating table and operated on him for apendicitis and it was nothing the matter there, so they opened the other side and there was nothing the matter there. Well, he lived two days after that and the doctors just kept at the poor little soul just as long as there was a breath in his poor little body and after he was dead. They decided he had paralysis of the bowels. Well, then they shipped him back to Hemet and they started back in the car and Bryce and Eleanor both sick they thought with the same ailment that Bobbie had. Warren after being up all the four nights and days drove the car all the way home without a stop. About 31 hours on the road. Poor kids! Myrtle was all in too. They had tire trouble too and in stopping to mend a tire they were so sick, over come with the heat of the desert, loss of sleep till Myrtle and Bryce began to have fainting spells, and in such grief. They let Bobbie's little dog out of the car and forgot her and lost her. They got home 2 O'clock Tuesday morning and Bobbie was buried at 3 o'clock Wednesday afternoon. We had all the arrangements made for them. We got Bro. Gold from Riverside and they brought two singers. They are so good down there at Riverside, and Bro. Gold gave a beautiful sermon on the resurrection. Warren chose the plot next to Daisy. When they got home that night it was certainly heartrending. Warren and Myrtle both broke down and cried and sobbed like two children. I can never forget it as long as I live and it cost Warren all he had and he owes over 400 dollars yet.

Well, no matter what happens, we have to look out for those who are left, and while waiting for this Arizona job we worked in the apricot orchard. Warren got to be a tray carrier and did pretty well and Myrtle was a fast worker at the pitting table but she did not feel well and kept feeling worse so Warren took her to Riverside and the doctor said she would have to have an operation for hemeroid piles, before she would be any better. So, we took her to the Community Hospital and she was opertated on; and they found an ulcer up high in the colon bowel and that made the operation worse. She was in hospital five days and then they brought her home. She had not gone to the hospital yet where they Fay's crowd got their orders to go to Arizona. So as soon as we dared to bring her we brought her. Warren was none to well and she not able at all to do for the family. Opal wanted to come out on a vacation to Papa, Opal and I and Harmon of couse came with them. Papa and I came in Opals car and Warren drove his car. We are here at the camp in Arizona not twenty rods from the brink of the Grand Canyon they did not tell it all. They are simply gorgeous. Opal and Myrtle was wishing for you and Luella to day. Ted and Helen live in less than three rods of us, but she acts so funny Opal and Myrtle have decided to let her alone. Ted is all right and has a good job and as far as I know is doing well. Ralph came with the crowd when they came but he did not get the job he wanted and is not satisfied. I don't know when we will get back home but Ralph says he is going back the 10th when some more boys are going back. Well, I must close and see if I can help with the supper. I will write to Luella next and will tell her about our trip.

So good by love to all tell Ellen and Lavinia
to write from your loving mother
Minnie E. Powell
Address Grand Canyon, Arizona
care of Pearson Dickerson camp

Romoland Calif.   Sept-10-1927

Dear Ruth, Wyman, Ellen and Lavinia

Your card and check enclosed came to hand a few days ago and I herewith enclose many thanks for the same. We was without a nickel in the house. Opal is doing all she can but she has a heavy load with her own family and worrying over papa and I. It is letting on her. She is growing thin faced and she carrys a worried look all the time. Fay had a job there at San Jacinto, but they wanted him to do a couple hours work as overtime lifting heavy sacks of feed and storing it in the loft of the feed barn. Fay asked if they payed for overtime and they said, ok. Fay said, Dammed if I work over time either. And he quit right there. Jobs are not very plentiful but he will find one, he always does. And then if they don't try to put upon him he is all right. If they do he will quit.

Wednesday the 14

95

Well I did not finish my letter the 10th so I will add a few more words tonight. I suppose you know Warren and family are back on the Bay by this time. We got a card from poor old Warren; he said they had a hard trip home, and it seemed so lonesome up there without Bobbie. Warren is so heartbroken over Bobbie's death. I can't think of him and keep the tears from coming. He has a nice little family left but he seems too heartbroken to realize it yet. Elinore is just as sweet and cute and smart as a child can be. It would surprise you to hear her tell about Bobbie. How he took sick and how they went to Flagstaff and how the Doctor operated on him and how he died and they shipped him to Hemet to where Daisy is and all about it and remembers the names of the towns and everything. I sure think she's a wonder. I wonder if June and Bryce have started to school up there. Harmon has started up to San Jacinto. Ralph has not started yet. It seems they have to put up 4 dollars to start in High School and are supposed to get it back at the end of the term if they don't smash up something or get away with their books or something.

Thursday. I didn't finish last night so will try again. Our next door neighbor's dog is barking till it sets us crazy. Ralph threatens to give him a feed of lead. I got your package of crochet work tonight. Thanks. And don't think I have forgotten the things I was going to send to you. I will get it done some of these days. Have patience. Papa has been having a bad week with his leg. It gathered and broke twice in the one week. I have been trying to get up to Hemet to the cannery. But things was in such a mess here I have been trying to clean up a little before I go. There won't be more than three weeks more after this week, but there is the roses that they want women workers for but I don't know what that work is. There is nothing left in Romoland now. The company has sold all this land and now they have shut down the Hall and the kitchen, they don't do any more irrigating for this year and have turned off most all the men, and now they have a tract up in Arizona. Well the way Judge Rutherford talks it certainly won't be long till things will begin to change. But the time of trouble must come first. I saw in a paper the other day that the World war started with trouble with the Balkans, and they are having trouble now with, I think, Germany. The first shot was liable to be fired any day.

Friday—16.

Well once more I will add a few more words to this queer letter and then I guess I will quit for this time. I have been working early and late and overtime trying to get a little order mixed in with this confusion. And I have got some of it done; but I don't think I will have it all done by Sunday. And I wanted to do some work out in the flowers, too. That cactus you brought down has had, I suppose a 100 blossoms on it this summer. It is going to bloom right away again now. The red hot poker has a blossomstock about a foot and a half high now and the red is showing in the blossom. That makes me think of Daisy. She planted it right out in front of the kitchen window so I could always see it, and remind me of the flowers at home—on Coos Bay.

I wish you could be down here now for a few weeks if I stay at home and maybe we could do some sewing. Or I would like to be up there with you and do some sewing up there. I don't think we will tie ourselves very closely to the place now that Daisy is gone.

Papa's leg is acting pretty bad too. Maybe he won't be here either. Well I guess I had better close for now. And I hope to hear from you soon.

Tell Ellen and Lavinia grandma sends lots of kisses and love and for them to write again. We read in the paper that Wyman fell and threw his sholder out of joint and that you set it and did a good job. I hope he gets along all right and tell him not to let it happen again.

From your loving Mother
Minnie Powell
Romoland
Calif.

Romoland Calif.   Sept-10 — 1927

Dear Ruth, Wyman, Ellen & Lavina
Your card and check enclosed came to hand
a few days ago and I ~~the~~ herewith enclose many
thanks for the same. We was without a nickel
in the house. Opal is doing all she can but she has
a heavy load with her own family and worrying
over papa and I. It is telling on her. She is growing
thin faced and she carrys a worried look all the
time. Fay had a job there at San Jacinto, but they
wanted him to do a couple hours work as overtime
lifting heavy sacks of feed and storing it in the loft
of the feed barn. Fay asked if they payed for overtime
and they said no. Fay said, Damned if I work over
time either. And he quit right there. Jobs are not
very plentiful but he will find one, he always does
And there if they don't try to put upon him he.
all right. If they do he will quit.

Photocopy of handwritten Minnie Powell letter (september 10, 1927) from Romoland, California

Wednesday the 14 — Well I did not finish my letter the 13th so I will add a few more words to-night. I suppose you know Warren and family are back on the Bay by this time. We got a card from poor old Warren; he said they had a hard trip home, and it seemed so lonesome up there without Bobbie. Warren is so heartbroken over Bobbie's death. I can't think of him and keep the tears from coming. He has a nice little family left but he seems too heartbroken to realize it yet. Elinore is just as sweet and cute and smart as a child can be. It would surprise you to hear her tell about Bobbie. How he took sick and how they went to Flagstaff and how the Doctor operated on him and how he died and they shipped him to Hemet to where Daisy is and all about it and remembers the name

Photocopy of handwritten Minnie Powell letter (september 10, 1927) from Romoland, California

of the towns and everything. I sure think she
~~think she~~ is a wonder. I wonder if Irene and Joyce [Boyce]
have started to school up there Harmon has started
up to San Jacinto. Ralph has not started yet. It
seems they have to put up of dollars to start in
High School and are supposed to get it back at the
end of the term if they don't smash up some
thing or get away with their books or something.
Thursday. I didn't finish last night so will try agai
Our next door neighbor's dog is barking till it sets us
crazy. Ralph threatens to give him a feed of lead. I got
your package of crochet work to night. Thanks. And
don't think I have forgotten the things I was
going to send to you. I will get it done some of
these days. Have patience. Papa has been having
a bad week with his leg. It gathered and broke
twice in the one week. I have been trying to get

Photocopy of handwritten Minnie Powell letter (september 10, 1927) from Romoland, California

up to Hemet to the cannery. But thing was in such a mess here I have been trying to clean up a little before I go. There wont be more than three weeks more after this week, but there is the roses that they want women workers for but I don't know what that work is. There is nothing left in Romoland now. The company has sold all this land and now they have shut down the Hall and the kitchen, they don't do any more irrigating for this year and have turned off most all the men, and now they have a tract up in Arizona. Well the way Judge Rutherford talks it certainly wont be long till things will begin to change. But the time of trouble must come first. I saw in a paper the other day that the World war started with trouble with the Balkans, and they are having trouble now with, I think, Germany. The first shot was liable to be fired any day.

Photocopy of handwritten Minnie Powell letter (september 10, 1927) from Romoland, California

Friday — 4. Well once more I will add a few more words to this queer letter and then I guess I will quit for this time. I have been working early and late and overtime trying to get a little order mixed in with this confusion. And I have got some of it done; but I don't think I will have it all done by sunday. And I wanted to do some work out in the flowers, too. That cactus you brought down has had, I suppose a 100 blossoms on it this summer, It is going to bloom right away again now. The red hot poker has a blossomstock about a foot and a half high now and the red is showing in the blossom. That makes me think of Daisy. she planted it right out in front of the kitchen window so I could always see it, and remind me of the flowers at home. — on Coos Bay. I wish you could be down here now for a few weeks if I stay at home and maybe we could do some sewing. Or I would like to be up there with

Photocopy of handwritten Minnie Powell letter (september 10, 1927) from Romoland, California

you and do some sewing up there. I don't
think we will tie ourselves very closely to the
place now that Daisy is gone.
Papa's leg is acting pretty bad too. Maybe he won't
be here either. Well I guess I had better close
for now. And I hope to hear from you soon.
Tell Ellen and Lavinia grandma sends lots
of kisses and love and for them to write again
We read in the paper that Wyman fell and threw
his sholder out of joint and that you set it
and did a good job. I hope he gets along all right
and tell him not to let it happen again
From your loving Mother.
Minnie Powell
Romoland.
Calif

Photocopy of handwritten Minnie Powell letter (september 10, 1927) from Romoland, California

Romoland, Calif.
Oct., 21 1927

Dear children:

Our and all grace and love be with you all is my Prayer we are all
alone just now. Ralph has gone down to store to find out about

picking grapes. He has to get work and so does Min. They have no car and cannot walk. It is to far and I don't know what will become of us. We thought we had our house and lot sold but the party told us to night they could not get the money and call it off. We have been hard off in our life but not like this. We always had enough to eat before they will sure take over our home if Min and Ralph don't get work. They talk going to Yuma and pick cotton, but cannot even get there. If we had a car and could go it would help us. Did you ever see Mary Burns man about that $2.00 for the calf we sold him? Don't know his name. Did Mrs. Clement get back home or go to jail? We never heard. She owes $11.85 and if she had it and knew our circumstances I know she would pay it. Well, I have wrote to you all 2 to 3 times and don't hear a word. Bro. Cole wrote me a letter and that is all guess. We are not worthy of notice or something. I don't know what is the reason. Why I have had one heck of a time with my leg. Sometimes I thought it would be all over for me, but it is better, but smells so I can hardly stand it and blood poisoning may start yet.

What is everybody doing? I see in Harbor Ted and wife got back to Coos Bay, they don't write. We have concrete sidewalks all over here and by our house. It is 85 to 96 in shade and we have not had a drop of rain. We are going to send you an invitation to start down here Ha, Ha. They sure got this valley cultivated in fine shape, one acre of grapes look fine. Grapes and peaches just rotted on the ground. We could get all we could haul to pick. We had all we could use. Lutz our neighbor brought by 5 large boxes of peaches and Min canned them. How is Warren? We heard he was not well, his head bothered him. But, don't mention this, so he would get hold of it as I think he suffers enough, poor fellow. I don't see how he ever drove over the road he did after Bobbie was shipped to Hemet being 5-days and nights and drive over the road in the night too. It was awfull and tire trouble to boot, it was a wonder he lived through it. So be sure about what I wrote and keep it still for his sake. I wrote him a letter and sent some spears of grass from Bobbie's grave, and told him of Min working in Cannery and Myrtle wrote and said he cried till midnight about it. And that Marina had to work as she was not able and he could not help us now. Min did have a sinking spell at Cannery, but went out in the air and got a cup coffee and got better. But we cannot do anything with her only let her have her way. She says she will work till she drops and it is all over before she will ask for money, for they all know how we are and if we can live on air we are the 1st ones that can. Now don't think we are or I am driving at you for I am not. Seems if I wrote to Luella she gets mad when I only write. As I would talk Fay and Opal have over paid us but they help us all they can, but Opal has not got the $100.00 of Daisy funeral during our summer sickness. They got behind $175.00 grocery and they have that to pay up and Opal looks bad and tired, not like she used to. Be worried because Mom has to work too. Fay has a job now at banning driving truck, road work. And I hope they will soon get caught up and so they would go on. We don't know who is next. Harmon was sick and had Doctor that is more expensive but is going to school this week.

Oct. 22 -

Well, just had breakfast and will try to finish this bunk. Ralph got a job picking grapes and we had to get up early to get him off as it is about 4 miles to walk. Well, I wish I could get a car, for Min a truck. So we could peddle like this tall one fellow picked peaches and bought some and took over to Glendale and sold them at $1.00 a crate and they did not cost him over $0.35 a crate, he would make $0.65 on $1.00 crates for two days work and small truck.

I figured coming to Coos Bay with about 250 crates and get maybe $1.25 a crate would clear about $200.00 a trip up there and then pick up a load of apples, potatoes, salmon, and butter and bring back and in all I think I could do that and make $300.00 clear a trip & 2 trips a mo. Would help us out. If we could keep our payments up until we could sell. Then we could see you all as we will ride on the truck and buy and sell.

So good by to all, specially to Ellen and Lavinia. I know they would write to us if they could. Love to all.

Grandpa

Dec. 29

Well, Opal I expect you were surprised when you got home the other night and found us gone. Well, we got home ok. Car ran good and came right along and that is all we expect it to do when we got it. Well, we found things pretty good though it rained awful here the night before we got here and things needed care to dry them and so on and the Lions Club had left us a box of grub at Yoders which we are glad to get. Warren sent us a small cheese 2 let Coos Bay cheese we got it last night. Several Christmas cards and such like.

Well, Opal if you can come down New Years will be glad we well be out of.

We are out of gas and all and oil and money even to buy. Or Ralph might come up, but don't like him to go till he gets his license to drive and be safe.

With love to all,
HP

San Jacinto, Calif.
Dec 30, 1927

Dear Ruth and Wyman also Ellen and Lavinia:

We got a great big pack in the mail yesterday and it was so big I had to get the to bring me home in his car so that I could see what I had and lo! and behold it was candy.

Well, we all feasted on chocolates, something we haven't had much of for 2½ years.

Harmon got a package 2 days before Xmas with a "chicken thief" in it. It and one other toy an erector set was all the more.

I am sorry that I did not send you folks some thing, but I just couldn't that's all. The folks came up here and I had turkey dinner for Xmas but I gave no presents to anyone except Harmon's $11.00 erector set.

I get quite discouraged at times. It's seems when I work as steady as I do I should have more and not be countinuously harping on being broke, but I can't seem to even keep even. If Fay worked as steady as I do, we might manage to keep even. But, the weather is bad and he has been off a whole week or more now.

My car is wore out and I haven't got the money nor inclination to have it fixed. It would cost more than it's worth.

I can't make a trip to Romolo any more and today I have a letter from Papa to get them some groceries. I get one every week. I give them on an average of $20.00 worth of groceries every month. It comes to about $5.00 a week and I don't see how they live on it. It costs four of us closer $40.00 a month and over. Last month they were up here a week during Thanksgiving and Christmas time. They came on Thursday and stayed until Monday. Ralph is not working and they are all out of clothes.

Please excuse me for rattling along this line but it is the thing uppermost on my mind these days.

I am going to mail you Papa's letter. Ralph says Mama cries most of the time. She don't know what to do. She just gets desperate I guess. She has wanted to get work and as she can't get around of course she don't get work.

Is Ed and Ted making anything? I haven't heard from them for a long time. I owe Ted a letter. I suppose they think it's good enough for me to have to help the folks. We came down here with them and we owed papa a lot.

Fay got a letter from the Indian Organization demanding his membership as he would not get any "Injun Money" if he didn't send it in. $6.50 up to Jan. and $1.50 per month. One could almost belong to the Masonic lodge for that price. I don't see how they could cheat him out of his legal share of an inheritance.

But the law does most anything. We haven't got no $5 membership fee nor are we paying $18 a year to stay a member. If the other Indians get their money and Fay does not, it's a rotten deal. The letter states that he should pay no money months in advance as possible to help more poor Indians that it pay. I'll tell them let some of the rich ones pay for the poor.

Gee guess I have run off at the face enough. That's what Fay would say, but he isn't here now. (I ought to write the Indian Organization that Fay is a "Coquille Injun" and that he don't get any money.

Well, guess you'll think I am getting hard boiled but I am not. I just got started off wrong. I don't feel half so bad as this sounds.

Some day if I can I will send you some oranges and walnuts and olives. But don't hold your breath till they come.

I may land another job and if I do, I'll send my mail here until you hear from me. I might be here several years you never can tell.

Hope you had a Merry Christmas and a Happy New Year. I hope the new year will be a prosperous one for you. Many thanks for the big box of candy.

With love and best wishes,
Opal

P.S.

What did Santa bring for Ellen and Lavinia?
  Aunt Opal

Romoland, Calif.
Jan. 19, 1928

Dear Ruth and Family:
  I expect you think I am not doing my duty in more ways than one; so I will try to redeem myself the best I can. If we could read the thought that go through the minds of those we love our understanding of each other would be so much better. I know I should have written a Christmas letter to all of you. And to you and Wyman in particular and thanked you for the Christmas rememberance it came in good for us too. I have of course heard of your Christmas and was glad you had a good time and a good dinner and then when we stop to think of more I think we have much to be thankful for. While we are no better than other people, we are always thankful when any thing sad or direful misses us. And I have heen truly thankful that the Infantile Paralysis has missed all of our little ones up there and pray they may wholey escape it, still we pray for the other little ones who are just as dear to their fathers and mothers and other friends as our are to us. What a sad old world it is! And what a happy world it will be when all this sickness pain and death is blotted out and all of earths millions are coming back and there will be no evil to make anyone afraid and all will be happy and healthy and all will be giving praises to the great and glorious King of earth, Almighty God.
  We can see the great Army in training for the last terrible battle almost everyday. The airplane service from March Field practices every day. They look so pretty too, up there in the air doing their stunts, but they could surely be an awful menace, too. If they were hostile. There is a big Army of men down there now and more coming. The first of the winter there was about 350 aviation students

came to March Field and now they are looking for about 280 more. The head ones of the aviation division of affairs are ordering more airplanes of different types. The heavier ones and lighter ones. The rules are awful strict after the boys once get in. They tell me there is a lots of unhappiness among them. They say one of them tried to jump out of an airplane the other day. The ages of them range from 15 up. Then there is bad ones and maybe some good ones. I don't know. Down where Ralph now is working they got on a frolic and came down and chased the men away from their job and would look over the side of their planes and laugh at them. They came down and frightened the team till the leaders broke loose from the machine and broke the harness all to pieces. They came down in the chicken yards and chased the chickens out of the yards and sent them flying everywhere.

Those on the ground felt like going to war and couldn't do anything. Those in the air was having a heighho time. The boss was going to report them to headquarters. Ralph said down there they left March Field in flocks 25 to thirty in a drove just like a flock of birds. Up here we only see one to four or five.

Ralph has got an old ford he paid ten dollars for it and has fixed it up so it takes him around to places where he hears of work and I go with him once in a while when there is need. Paps hasn't taken chances only a time or two. This job Ralph got this time he made about 40 dollars. He got himself some clothes and got some repairs for the car and gave us fifteen of it and then his old Lizzie balked. It took him and Archie Cowart two days to coax her to go. They are gone down there now to see if they have lost their job.

Since the first of January, it has been *cold*. It rained here for nearly a week and up in the mountains it snowed. When the fog cleared from the mountain tops they were white with snow. All the low mountains except these first low ranges were white to the valley level.

Old San Jacinto was white to the valley level and it snowed in San Jacinto. Of course it melted out of San Jacinto town in a few hours but here is plenty of snow in the mts. And as soon as the sun goes down it is cold. Garden stuff grows outside, but I don't. I get Ralph's breakfast and then curl up by the heater and stay there till the sun shines good and plenty before I stick my nose out of the kitchen. Do you take the Watch Tower? We just got ours today and pap has just finished the first article. It proves so continuously that God will demonstrate to the world almost now that he alone is Jehovah, that there is no other like him. We can almost see the picture of the new heavens and the new earth where in dweleth righteous. If anyone colporter comes in that country with the book be sure to get <u>Creation</u>.

It is the latest from Judge Rutherford pen. It is harder to drop it to do the work we should do than a fascinating love story. If you can get it, try it! Well, I guess I have written most all I know. Well gossip a little about the neighbors and then I will quit.

Mrs. Cowart is just the same good old neighbor. She got to go home to see her mother last summer. She was gone two months. She let Harry's folks have him in order to get the money to go on. When she came back she never rested until she got him back and then he and Ruthie fought like cats and dogs. She was glad to give him up. She took him back her self. Then they brought him back again and left him. She sure was sick of her bargain. She wrote them to come and get him, two or three times before they did come. Finally his mother came on the stage and took him with her. That is only two or three days ago. I think that will end her taking care of Harry.

Our neighbors on the other side of the street came home just after we came home from the Grand Canyon. You know where the old deaf man lived. Now he is bound the old lady shall marry him and she says she won't and he has threatened to shoot her and they are having a lively time.

Well, I received the check you sent and thank you and God bless you all. I am about to the end of my paper so I will choke off.

From your loving Mother,
Minnie Powell
Romoland, Calif.

Romoland, Calif.
Jan. 10, 1928

Dear Ellen,

When we received the letter from your mother the other day, we got a letter from Lavinia. We did not get a letter from you. I suppose you was busy getting supper or washing dishes or mending your doll.

The sun is shining just fine today. I expect you will beat me picking flowers though. The Daisies that grow in the grass I mean.

I hope you are well and will write soon. And I suppose you will be going to school soon.

From your loving Granmother.
Mrs. Minnie Powell
Romoland

Romoland, Calif.
Jan. 10, 1928

Dear Lavinia,

Grandpa and I received your letter a few days ago and was surely glad to hear from you. We read your letter through with much pleasure. Write again.

The sun is shining and the birds are singing and I put a pan of water out by the blackberry vine and they came there in big flocks to drink and bathe in the pan.

I hope this will find you well and Grandpa and I would sure like to see you and Ellen once more.

From your loving Granmother.
Mrs. Minnie Powell
Romoland

Romoland, Calif.
Feb. 27, 1928

Dear Ruth and Family. Wyman and Ellen and Lavinia:

I am a slow old polk but I get around occasionally, and now it is your turn and I will try to write something to you. There is nothing to write that is interesting but I will tell you about what we do here at home and so here goes.

Papa is much the same as usual. I don't think he can do a much at a time as he could last year. But he won't have as much to do.

We were threatened by the company that we would have to pay up or lose our contract. So we wrote to them and offered them the equity on our acre and the one lot to be applied on the lot we live on and just keep the one on which we live. They wrote right back that they would and we have their letter. So we wrote right back and sent back the old contract and asked them to make out a new contract on this lot but they have not done so yet. I was anxious that they should fix it up right away so we could begin making payment it only leaves 105 dollars to pay and then we would be through with land payments.

And I guess we could make it somehow. When we got back from Grand Canyon last fall, Papa and I put in three weeks work on these lots hoeing down the weeds drying and burning picking up rubbush and when Ralph got home from Yuma where he went to pick cotton he helped too. We tore down all the old goat and chick barns and fences and piled them up and we had it looking pretty decent around here. Then the company put paved sidewalks and it is pretty good. But the weather got cold and we used Daisy bedroom for a sitting room and hovered around the little heater and burnt up the wood out of the old sheds and the weeds and grass grew to suit themselves, and Ralph tinkered with old cans in the dooryard till it sure looked slummy. But in due time he got through and the old Chandler had disappeared and most of the old parts of cars are gone. Some of them are left but not many. A few of eucalyptus stumps and a hole he dug to drive the car over so he could work under it.

Papa has been putting in his time cutting the weeds and grass and planting garden. And he has got his part of it pretty again. My part in the front yard don't look so good. I worked out there one day and then I have been trying to straighten up the house and do some patching. But I'll work out there another day pretty soon. The old cactus that you brought was the prettiest thing all last summer. It blossom most all summer. Once it had seven blossoms most all the summer.

The two eucalyptus trees Wyman set out in the back yard is growing fine. They are all of 3½ feet high. And is sprout that I think they called a gum tree that some of them set out in from is ten or twelve feet high. I am not going to put out much time on flowers this year. I will try to take care of the Chrysanthimums that Daisy had and the bulbs.

I have sent for two agent outfits for a company to sell about the same goods as the Walk Rawliegh or McNess Companies. If I can do anything with it I will stay with it for a while. I have got to do something. I have tried all winter to land a job and I can't seem to make it. So I will try this. I have been looking for the sample case all the week. It came from Ohio. If it don't come pretty soon I guess I might have to go after it.

Papa and I are all alone. And have been for two weeks. Ralph went up to Opals to help Fay fix up Opals overland so she could ride to her work. They finished last night Friday. Then Opal had a chicken dinner on Sunday for Harmons birthday. His birthday was on Wednesday but she could not be home until Sunday. Then they took Ralphs ford and started out to find work. They must have struck a job for I have not heard from them and this is Friday.

After the 7th of April they expect to go up to the logging camps 70 miles from Fresno somewhere, but we will see what happens.

A man by the name of Cozine who was sick with T.B. when Daisy died the other day and one of his sisters is in the hospital at Riverside not excepted to last long. They came here from Colorado. Mrs. Cowan has a sister with her now who has T.B. She came here from Mississippi. She moves so much like Daisy used to. And she coughs so bad. They had the preacher and several others praying over her yesterday as they wanted to over Daisy when she was here. What a foolish Old World, and what a wicked Old World it is getting to be I suppose you have read the article from the IBSA about the war in Heaven in 1918 when Christ threw Satan out of Heaven with all his bad angels down to earth and that they are at large in the Earth till it is time for Satan to be bound for the thousand years. It surely seems that they are here don't it. Of all the fiendish deeds that are being committed. I don't think the like was ever heard of before. It surely behooves us to keep very close to our Lord to seek his protection in all the ways possible at all times. And when these evil spirits see the blood on the inlets of our doom that we are trusting in the precious blood of our Redeemer they will pass us by. The class at Riverside gave a little pamphlet to Papa on the studies of the Great Primid, that as near as we could understand meant a great change of some kind that would start on the 30th day of May 1928. It might be the start of Armegedden or it might be something concerning the little Flock Class. I could not just understand what. God help us all in any case. And may we all watch and be sober looking unto the coming of the Lord.

Well, it is late and I am getting cold and I will bid you good night and hoping to hear from you soon. And how we would like to see you all and we would like to see dear old Coos Bay of the surf.
From your loving mother.
Minnie Powell
Romoland, Calif
Box 9E

Weedpatch, Calif
Oct. 20, 1928

Dear Ruth and Family:

I have had you in mind for a long time but we have been in such a scrubbish ever since we got back to California that I did not know hardly when or how to start in.

Warren got some work in Romoland but Fay held out hope to him that he could get work at Pasadena for more money and he let go of Steve and then when work in Pasadena did not materialize and we heard about so much work out to Bakersfield especially picking cotton that he decided to come out here and try it. I wanted to come to try my luck in the cotton patch so against everybodys wishes and advice I am here and papa is at home. Of course he is a liability anyday and they all told me I could not stand the work and couldn't pick any if I could stand it. But I was determined to try and so I did and if something don't happen different they were all right and as usual I was all wrong I worked one day and a half and made about $1.20 I will try it again this afternoon I guess.

And if you hear of somebody making a fortune picking cotton down here, that is one of course there is not anything going smoothly these days. Roys mother is not so big as I am but she is a bigger old fool than three of me would make. She is absolutely crazy over an old widower that came into Romoland and he came out to pick cotton and she had to stick along to be with him and I had to ride with them and sleep with her and we was all messed up with our cooking till we landed here in this cotton patch and then Warren took the bits in his teeth and set up his own tent and let them go it. But I have had to go over there to sleep till last night. Then I bucked and stayed in Warrens tent.

Well, she came over early this morning for June to come over and stay with her till she could cook breakfast forlorn. So I guess I will have to go back to Chfstemr the darned old fool to help June out.

Warren and Myrtle have not done well yet picking cotton and the kids are begging to go back to Oregon. I don't know how they will make it, maybe they will get more used to it and can do better. There are some in the field who came picking 3 or 4 hundred a day, at so per hundred. That is pretty good. If I could do half that well I would kill myself right in the but there is no danger I guess.

Well, this is all I know and then some. So I will quit for this time. If you write address to Romoland. Love to Ellen and Lavinia and all of Luellas folks and yourself.

From Mama

Romoland, Calif.
Nov. 16th, 1928

To Wyman & Ruth & Ellen & Lavinia
Am going to try to write you a line & half if find you all well and happy.

We are anything but happy. I don't know what will become of us. & Min is cross & I begin to feel like I would welcome my rest beyond the vail. I cannot see why but it is so & tonight we got a bill of $32.00 for water & that would cut it off if not paid in 5 days. Ralph has gone over to tell them he would work it out but we have no money and most everybody sick just now and we will have to call on county. Min says she stay right here & starve it out and I will too.

Warren is better but not well but got his life insurance and paid me and at Terra Bella Calif. picking oranges & many do pretty well. If kids about be sick all the time I think they had difftheria and the flu hope they are all better some. If Warren gets sick they all come down sick too.

Fay and Opal have been guaranteed for quite a while for Harmon had it & got over it and started to go to school and then they sent him home and told Opal to get a doctor and she has and I have not heard from her since. Min is entirely broke down she was bound to go with Warren to Bakerfield and just played out. Is too hard work and we all argued against it but she had her way but I stayed here and batched. It was close rigging but I made it but Opal made $3.00 picking cotton and cost about $9.00 to get up and back but she has frailed right along since she got home and I don't know what to do. The Lord be our guide. We have put our trust in the lord for a long time and still trust in his care. There is not any work around here at present but the Co. say things will stand 1st year. Hope so Warren was coming here to work after got through up there but we had a letter from them in which they said they are getting onto the Orange picking and so may get in down here when they come back. Well Ralph just come and said they would give him a card to work at another place and they would not turn the water off for us. So much we won't choke for a drink, yet for a while. My cough all left and Min got better till she will that cotton picking and if she would rest and with Patrick I think she may still come out of it hope so for I don't know what we would do with her sick out here and Opal has to work. She certainly has stayed with all of us through thick and thin. We had planned on an auto when we came back & go in the colportuer work that has stopped for now at least we must try.

Some kind peanut started or something I don't know. Well I expect you will be tired of this sheet and writing but I only got 4 stamps and it may be along time before I can write again hope you all a good thanks given dinner may the lord bless you all in my prayers.

H. Powell

Romoland, Jan. 19th 1929

Well Wyman & Ruth - Ellen & Lavinia. Hello dear ones I would of wrote you long ago but was down with the flu & was broke too not even a postage stamp to write. I had a book of stamps but could not find until your letter came & Min wanted me to write the Co. for her about the lot & in look for some papers. I found my stamps Ha Ha. & as it is stormy out I thought I would write you all the best. It is hard for me too write. Yet I was sick & when I did get better did not have what my appetite wanted & when I swallowed, it gave me the hickups real bad but is better now. Opal sent me a bottle flu medicine they use over there & it helped me great but we have had a time of it.

Well we was glad you sent that PO order as it will help wonderfully thanks a thousand times or more.

Warren & family will be on Coos Bay before you get this if nothing hapens. Then we got letter from him & they expected to camp at Dunsmier last night & go over to Ashland to day. I hope they get through all right.

They tryed hard to make it here but seems like everything was against them. So you will see them. So I will not try to write it. I planted cabbage & tomatoes seed this morning it is too cold for garden truck to grow much at this time year but when sun shines it is warm.

Well Min has just started on foot to post office. I tried to get her to be ready sooner and catch a car but she wont listen to it & now she will be done up all day tomorrow. It is too far for her & she cannot go like she use to no more. I have no more to write as news are dull but your shade trees are fine. You will have to come & tap them & let them branch out more. So good by & write often. May the *Lord* bless you all.

    H. Powell
        Romoland
            Calif.

Well Miss Ellen Albee how do you do. That name sounds like a school girl I know & really I think it is the same one she lives at Cape Argo Light House & goes to the Charleston School. Do you think that is her. Where do you live & do you go to school like that girl I know. Write & tell me & do you speak pieces in school & tell the others scholars how & so, so. Well Ellen gran Pa has been quite sick & could not write to his little friends but now maby he will. Keeping on getting well & then you will hear from him more. Gran Ma just got back from PO & Mrs Cowart told her to come & get in her car & go to Perris & she could get some things at the Chain Store & save a few dimes & so she went & have not got back yet. So I will have to say good by & pray the Lords blessing upon you. Write soon,

    from Gran Pa

Well now I have got right up to everybodys girl Miss Lavinia Albee. How do you do & especially when Ellen is to school & you all alone. What do you do all day. You cant catch crabs & clams or fish but I bet dady can though if he aint much of a trapper. Well I was glad to hear from you all. I work in garden some but it is stormy at times disagreable to be out. So I stay in house now till the weather gets better & I get more well. Dont want no more flu in mind. I am going to look for you to come & see me & I will plant some mellons so you can have plenty & if in season all the grapes you can eat all the time you are here. Well Gran Ma has just got back from Perris & acts quite spry. Hope it does her good & now she says for a square meal & I. So good by my good girl & write often. May the Lord bless you.

H. Powell
Romoland, Calif.

Romoland California   1-20-1929

Dear Ruth and All The Family,

We received your welcome letter yesterday morning. I guess we have to give Lavinia the credit; as she started things. We were glad to hear you were all feeling well. Tell Ellen she must get over her cold or it is liable to develope into the flu. This winter has been the limit for the flu down here. I did not have it much. I coughed some for awhile, but it did not hurt me any. Papa had quite a siege but he is getting all right now. If he doesn't get a backset. The weather has not been very good pretty near all the week. Cloudy and rained some. Cold too, I have hovered over the stove most all the week and refused to keep house till it was warmer. Today it is the climax I guess. It rained pretty near all night and has rained most of the time today. A cold rain. Yesterday when your letter came it found us out of everything in grocery line, milk, butter, meat, coffee, lard, etc., and just 6¢ between us. Do you doubt that we were glad to get your letter and the check you sent us. Thanks till you are better paid. And the calander, how did you know just what we wanted? Papa had just wished in the morning that he had a calendar with big figures that he could see across the room. Thanks for that too.

The payment on the lot was over due and I went down and sent the payment on its way and when I came back Cowarts was just going to Perris with their car and let me go along and I got a nice bill of groceries and thank you for that. Warren and Myrtle have been to Opals since two weeks ago. He could not get anything to do here and Annie wrote that the Mills and camps was all starting up there and they decided they would go back to the Bay. Myrtle was not feeling well and the weather none to good so they only started last Thursday. We got a letter from them yesterday that they expected to stay in Dunsmire, that would have been Friday night.

So they may have made it lucky up there. They just could not make it so get in anywhere.

Poor old Myrtle did all she could do and put up with all kinds of circumstances to make ago of it. But they couldn't make it.

We worried about their going over the mountains this time of the year. But if nothing has happened they must be home by this time. But we will be uneasy until we hear they are there.

I expect we will be in the garden to set out and my front yard is in need of all kinds of work. It was to bad that your pretty little goat did not turn out as well as you expected but that was my luck. I could write on and on but this has to go in with papas letter and I have to write to Luella right now for this is two letters to you since I wrote to her. Tell Ellen and Lavinia that they can look for a letter from grandma soon all of them.

And love to you all and good bye for this time. From your loving mother.

Minnie Powell - Romoland, Calif,. Box 108

Romoland, Calif.
June 1, 1929

To Ruth and Wyman, Ellen & Lavinia,
Gosh that is a long name…

How are you four & I hope you are well & happy. We are not very well, but not complaining.

Min has just gone and layed down for a while until time to get supper. Ralph is working irrigating crew today. He has been working steady but the pay comes slow, he has two paydays and today is on the 3rd but he looks for some soon now, hope so. I work in garden all I can & it is good. Will have mellons and tomatoes and grapes galore by August. When you come down and all other garden truck in plenty about 300 cabbage and my rutabaggas are doing well but can't say how they will come out. I have about 1000 head lettuce doing well. Tho' Co. gave us a lot of fig cutting if we would clean it all up and Ralph & Woodrow halled them up & in the bottom where didn't shifted down these was green & they told us to plant them & Co. would give us 1500 a piece next year for all that grow & Min set out eighteen hundred & hope they do well so I can get a shirt & pair overalls if I am here. Have to put that in as things are so uncertain one cannot tell.

We got about 6 tier wood out of it & Mr. Lutz said he will see we get some heavy wood to go with it. Now if we can get a stove to burn it. We will be pretty well fixed.

Next winter we want to get what they call wash room and laundry stove with 4 holes on top of and would be cook & heater combined & would save oil lots of time too.

Opal wrote and said you all wanted us to meet them at Roseburg the 9th of July but we cannot get away. Would loose all our stuff besides Min and Ralph will be in the fruit if she can get work she can do. I tell you we got to do something or go naked and that would not be very nice. Min says well if we come we will have to get cloths around & we would not want to take such a trip with a few dollars of our own in all we figure it would take about $40.00 now I am only explaining & not asking for money but just to tell you the circumstances Opal and Fay & Doc may go but their car is not large enough either to take us all.

So will have to stay we cannot go would be glad to see you all it would be so good but what can't be cured will have to be endured. If we sell out & fix so we can we will see you all again before we get tied up again.

I wrote Luella a letter the other day & forgot a lot of this & so will ask you to take this over & read both together.

I cannot write like I used to. I think I will then. I just cannot think of anything at all.

Roy Graham's folks are up around Sacremento picking cherries they may go to Coos Bay if he does, he not to take him on a deer hunt he cannot keep from talking & tell all about what you done & not mean any harm at all but to bragg on you, I could cite a case here but won't now & we all like them. I joked him about taking me too Coos Bay & he would not talk about it he has a young married couple with them & Mattie told me she was tired and wanted to get a home and settled.

And that was a lot for her to say but I think she has a big share to do for sake of having the couple & see they only come to see us a few minutes.

Well, would be glad to hear from you all what of how is Warren making it? I hope good and will save and get a stand once again.

Well good bye and the Lord be with you, you are in my prayers.

H. Powell

Jan. 30, 1930
Romoland, Calif.

Dear Children, Wyman, Ruth, Ellen, and Lavinia one and all:

The love of Christ be with you, all is in my prayers.

We read your welcome letter & it was a comfort to hear from you once more. We sent your check as our last payment on our lot but don't mention it up there it will cost us about $16.00 more for abstract & recording we expect but it is home. There is no place like home let it be ever so humble.

We have had a nice winter up to about 10 days ago & it begun to storm & we laughed & said Wyman must be coming Ha Ha. Well, the country needed rain & we have got it in plenty. But like Coos Bay it don't seem to know when to stop.

We got a new stove & roll paper & fixed our front room up so we have had it very comfortable this winter. The trouble it is so hot for so long there is not a roof in town knows enough to shed water & so we all experience the rain together until the shingles get wet & swell up & the holes in tar paper get full of dirt & then they shed water pretty good.

Opal & Fay came out yeaterday Sunday to see how we were getting along through the storm. They had quite a cold trip but made it out all right, it is 80 miles & they don't have long to stay but are busy visiting while they are here. Roy Graham & family live just across the street at present. Roy said he was a going to write you for a job during your vacation. I don't suppose it would be any use for me to ask for Barkers place like I had. I always felt I did not give the satisfaction that was looked for. Well the *Lord* is with us all & so far we will make the best of it.

Minnie says she would not go visiting again while she could work in cannery & get our bills paid. We owe $35.00 on lumber yet she paid half of it last year & says if she is able will make the rest this year is why I have wrote the above which would help us pay the bill & then some & we could make a visit. Besides Ralph took Fays car & went up to Nuevo where he worked in Onions & bought the nicest big sack of onions for $1.25 about 120 lbs of them. Opal paid for them & gave us half. Our hens have begun to lay. We will have about 32 hens to lay but one eat an egg yesterday & that means chicken in the pot with dumplins. Well it may come out ok yet Min is trying to wash in the kitchen but she is not well. She got the flu & it tells on her & slow to get over it. What you think 1930 will bring forth. The world seems to be in a terrible state trying to get where they can say peace & safety then suden distruction. Well have no more to write & will say write soon it is a great day to get your letter. God be with you in my wishes.

Good By

    H. Powell

WHERE'S THE OLD KEEPER

The bustling breeze has ceased for a rest,
The billowing sea stops the heave of her breast;
White clouds unfurl like sails late at night,
But where's the old keeper who looks after the light?

A gull is at rest on the lighthouse tower,
A ship floats along like a drifting flower.
The fish are swimming around for a bite,
But where's the old keeper who looks after the light?

The sun sinks low, the night draws near,
The voice of the keeper we cannot hear.
A flag is fluttering on the mast half height,
But where's the old keeper who looks after the light?

The sun has set in the golden West,
The honest keeper has done his best,
Stars are twinkling and shining bright;
But where's the old keeper who looks after the light?

Ila Albee

About the Author

Mrs. Lee has retired on beautiful Bainbridge Island, Washington, surrounded by the natural beauty of the Pacific Northwest and Puget Sound region. A day's trip in any direction will take her to the Olympic Mountains or the Pacific Coast or the Cascades, Mount Rainier or Northwest Trek – a reserve of the wild animals of the Northwest.

Mrs. Lee grew up along the coast of Oregon and the San Juan Islands of Washington as a child of a lighthouse keeper during the Great Depression and during World War II. Her experiences growing up around the different light stations are unique, and are captured in time in this book, *Children of the Lighthouse*.